Gary G. Fallon & Kathy A. Fallon

Separated...
but Not Divorced

7 Painful Pitfalls
to Avoid

Llumina Press

Requests for permission to make copies of any part of this work should be mailed to Permissions Department, Llumina Press, PO Box 772246, Coral Springs, FL 33077-2246

ISBN: 978-1-59526-440-4

Printed in the United States of America by Llumina Press

Library of Congress Control Number: 2006905545

To You.

Who are now *separated but not divorced,*
this book is dedicated. What to do next
is why this book is in your hands.

Table of Contents

Preface

You're separated but not divorced. *Now what?* It's a question I asked myself over and over when I was going through the same thing. How I answered that question greatly impacted my life and everyone around me.

The same will be true for you. That's why this book was written - to help you answer the *Now what?* question. *Your* answer, will be life-changing.

I eventually learned how to answer that question. In part, it's due to my own lessons learned *after* my marriage of eighteen years, which included three great kids. It was then that I found myself separated. My former wife decided she wanted out. I fought it every way I could, but in the No-Fault state of Florida, it only takes one person to see a marriage end. She eventually married the guy she was engaged to when our divorce was final. As for myself, I went through approximately seven years as a separated, then divorced, single-again Christian father.

On the other hand, Kathy, my present wife and co-author of this book, experienced separation differently than I did. During fifteen years of marriage, which included two great kids, she had prolonged her marriage in hopes that her husband would make real changes in his lifestyle. After years of seeing no permanent change and with biblical grounds for divorce, she filed. He's been married two more times during the additional fifteen years Kathy remained a separated, then divorced, single-again Christian mother.

So how can we be so sure that the pages you are about to read will change your life? Well, in our own lives, after experiencing both separation and divorce, we personally fell into each of the *7 Pitfalls* we are about to share. We didn't know ahead of time they were there, but we learned about them as time went on. And learning the hard way is just that - the *hard* way. The painful way, the damage-yourself-and-others-along-the-way way. It's not only because of our own experiences, but because of the lives of hundreds of others we've met through years of Separation/Divorce Recovery Ministry that we know being aware of these *7 Painful Pitfalls* can truly change your life. If you are kept from experiencing what Kathy and I went through, what hundreds of thousands of others have gone through, you will know what we mean when we say, *"What you are about to read will change your life."*

How or why you are separated is *not* what this book deals with. Those issues are important, but that's not why we wrote this book. The fact is, you're here: *Separated—But Not Divorced.* Now that you *are* here, our goal is to help you along this journey. We've approached our task with a twist, weaving testimonials throughout each chapter. It's proved to be extremely helpful when presenting these *7 Painful Pitfalls To Avoid* for those in marital separation.

These testimonies are a compilation of real people's experiences, derived from hundreds of personal and small-group discussions with separated and divorced Christians—including ourselves—over a combined fifteen-year time span, with added literary expressions to enhance each representation. Variations of each story could be echoed over and over from city to city by those who have or are presently experiencing marital separation. This writing style is our way to help you to identify with those who are experiencing the same things you are experiencing and who have first-hand knowledge of the key principles being discussed in each chapter. Although names, locations, and details have been altered to maintain anonymity, these are *their* stories. Many may represent *your* story.

Introduction

(*Pit-fall*)

1. An unapparent source of trouble or danger; a hidden hazard: "potential pitfalls stemming from their optimistic inflation assumptions."[1]
2. A concealed hole in the ground that serves as a trap.
3. An unforeseen or unexpected difficulty.[2]

These *7 Pitfalls* are real. There are people, who have traveled this road of separation before you, and a lot of them fell into a lot of these *pitfalls*—and they care enough to warn you. Some of these things most people were unaware of or didn't want to believe when they were separated, but now, looking back, they have learned. They are ahead of you on the road.

This book is a starting point, a road map with signs stating what's up ahead around the next bend. You are on this journey of separation, and, as mentioned earlier, *why* or *how* you got here is not the emphasis of this book. It's to help you now that you're here. You may have been on the journey for one week, one month, one year, or longer, but you're here, like it or not. This really is happening.

There is a better way to travel on this journey, though. That's why this is in your hands. Either you or someone who cares about you felt you could benefit from its contents. And you *will* benefit from it in ways you've yet to discover. The benefit starts by becoming aware of the general pitfalls themselves, which are stated as the title of each chapter. But understanding a particular pitfall really comes by reading the entire chapter—not just glancing at titles.

Will you agree with everything you read? Possibly not, at least not now, but maybe later on you will come to see things in a different light. I know that was true for Kathy and me and thousands of others. Should not agreeing with every pitfall stop you from digging deep into each one? Of course not. That being said, we suggest that, as you read, you approach each pitfall with an open mind, saying to yourself, *"I may or may not agree with this, but I'll consider it."* Some of you will do more than consider it; you will actually *change* because of these warnings. But no matter where you stand, Kathy and I are asking, hoping, and praying that you read each one with an open mind.

Thanks for the privilege of being your guides in describing the road ahead. We've been where you are right now, as has everyone who contributed to this book. The journey is not really understood by those who have never traveled it. Many friends, relatives, and co-workers have *heard* of the road of separation and give their advice to you, with great sincerity and some with strong conviction—you know exactly whom I'm talking about—but unless they have traveled it themselves, they don't *really* understand.

Even those who *have* traveled it might have fallen into every pitfall and can't even identify what it was they experienced. This book is about those who, through their failures and successes, *can* clearly identify and explain what is ahead—and what the pitfalls are like. Their stories and insights await you.

A Support Group?
Not Now, Maybe Later

◆ ◆ ◆

W hat about you? Have you ever considered joining a support group? Most *separated but not divorced* Christians don't even think of or hear about this option. That's the *Pitfall*. They don't consider it or they put it off—*"Not now, maybe later."*

But it's a gold mine of an opportunity. Although there are some support groups available through a licensed counselor or therapist, these are likely to cost quite a bit of money, and most are only available in secular settings. Beneficial? Of course, to a degree. But for Christian views with a biblical perspective, nothing can beat *DivorceCare*, a great ministry to those who are in either the separation phase or the divorce phase. Both types of people are ministered to in this biblically based support group, and we have found that nearly half or more of the attendees at most DivorceCare seminars are in the separation phase.

In 1993, Steve Grissom, who found himself divorced with nowhere to turn, decided to create his own video-oriented divorce recovery support group. His professional background was media, so he interviewed on videotape: ministers, Christian counselors, and actual participants in his early DivorceCare support groups.

The end product was a video-taped series where each session would include watching a video, followed by a small group question and answer period covering content presented in the video. A seminar workbook with video outline notes and Bible studies was also provided.

Christians everywhere started hearing about the success of the program, which primarily met and still meets in local churches. Now, over a decade later, Steve Grissom has re-created an even more compelling series with the release of the updated DVD format, which provides additional topics, testimonies, and informative graphics for today's Separated and Divorced.

Nancy hadn't even heard of DivorceCare until a friend invited her to the one she was attending at a local church.

"It was such an incredible experience to walk in and find everyone, literally everyone in the room was either separated or divorced. These were people who I

could relate to and knew exactly what I was going through! The videos showed people just like me going through separation, and the small-group discussion afterwards was incredibly real and brought clarity to my own situation."

Nancy – Chicago, IL

Walker had never been to any kind of support group for anything in his life and felt it could help "others"— but him?

"I was still a little skeptical about going, but saw the ad in my local newspaper, and after receiving a brochure in the mail about it, decided if it could help me, even a little, I should be open to it. I knew I was messed up over all this separation stuff and wasn't sure what to do. Arriving at the local church was a bit of a stretch for me, especially since I hadn't been to any church for a long time! But the church was just hosting DivorceCare, and I was pretty sure I wasn't going to get pressured to become active at the church. I was there for a specific reason: to help get my head and life back on course, to hopefully get some direction and suggestions for this new phase of my life. I wasn't wrong—about the church or the goals I had hoped to achieve there! To think I was so hesitant when now I'm getting so much!

Walker – Atlanta, GA

There are other support groups besides DivorceCare, but those with the aid of a video series make a major difference. Christians experiencing separation and divorce seem to think so, too! Over 12,000 churches of nearly every denomination, in all fifty states and in over twenty countries around the world, have utilized DivorceCare. The seminar sessions are free, some with only a minor cost for a workbook. Many also provide childcare, so you can place your small children in the care of church attendants until your seminar session is over.

The program is set up so you can join it at any time. Each session is self-standing, so you don't need to attend the previous ones to understand it. When I first encountered DivorceCare for myself, I began in Week 3. I simply continued through the following sessions and came back through to pick up the ones I missed. Some of the topics found in the DivorceCare seminars include: [1]

* What's Happening to Me?
* Single Sexuality
* New Relationships
* Financial Survival
* The Road to Healing / Finding Help
* Forgiveness
* What Does the Owner's Manual Say?
* KidsCare
* Facing Your Anger, Facing Your Depression, Facing Your Loneliness

The unique approaches to each of these and other topics are especially rewarding for those who have come to seek real answers and guidance.

"During my first visit at our DivorceCare class, I arrived a little early. As I sat in my seat, I began to glance through the workbook that came with the seminar. The topics were so where I was at! The table of contents read like my life over the previous four

months! When the video finally started, it seemed like I was watching myself up on the screen. The testimonies of people just like me were giving us their story as it related to the specific topic for that day. I was so drawn into them describing their feelings, their choices, their outcomes.

"It's been six months since I completed those thirteen-week sessions. The timing for me was what DivorceCare was all about. The timing and the topics. They went hand in hand. Until you go through it yourself, you really don't see it. All I know is, what I needed to hear came at the right time!"

Tyrone – Greenville, SC

"I convinced myself that the subject to be discussed that week in DivorceCare was not for me. I wasn't in the 'Anger' stage. Hurt, yes. Deep anger, no. Never had been and wasn't now—so why go? I would definitely go the following week; I needed to hear more about that one, but not about 'Anger.' My soon-to-be ex could really use this week's topic! He was the King of Anger! That was a big part of why we got separated in the first place. I got glimpses of it when we were dating, but we were so 'in love' that I was convinced I'd love that anger right out of him. Boy, was I stupid!

"Anyway, we dated much too short of a time to really deal with issues like anger. We had wedding plans to take care of! It was your classic rush-to-the-altar-type wedding. All our friends said, 'Slow down,' but we kept saying, 'This is different, and when you know what you want and you see it in front of you, why play the waiting game?' Well, we didn't play that game, and we got married within seven months of meeting each other. Stupid. That's what it's called.

Just plain stupid. Now, we're separated after only two years of marriage.

"*Anger? He needed this week's class, not me. But guess what? I did end up going. If it hadn't been for one of the other girls in my small group calling me and encouraging me to go, I would have missed one of the best classes for me at DivorceCare! The topic uncovered aspects of anger I had no clue about. I discovered 'hidden anger' traits about myself that, after the video, were anything but hidden! I saw things I was doing that were clearly outcomes of deep, covered anger within me. It was so clear to me that I thought it not possible to have learned so much about me! I put on such a non-angry face and manner with everyone around me. Me, angry? No way. Yes way. Only, it didn't have the same appearance that my husband exhibited. But it was still there, deep within me.*

"*I'm sure there have been many like me, judging the session's content by its topic title. I didn't make that mistake again. I committed myself to going every week whether or not I thought I 'needed' that topic in my life or not!*"

Laura – Los Angeles, CA

To learn more, you can visit their user-friendly Web site at **www.DivorceCare.org**. While you're there, you can locate the group nearest your zip code. It's fast and easy. The "*Find a Group*" icon is right on the front page. Clicking that takes you to a page that provides a box for you to enter your zip code. You choose the radial distance from your house (five, ten, twenty, thirty, fifty, even up to one hundred miles from you). Most cities have a variety of meeting locations. Calling the host church to get the Group Leader's name, phone number, and meeting time is simple.

You won't regret going online, finding a location, and attending!

WIDE USE OF SUPPORT GROUPS

Support groups of any kind, be it for separation and divorce, cancer, or drug addictions, have always proved helpful. The very definition of *support group* identifies the potential benefits:

(Support group n.)

1. A group of people, sometimes led by a therapist, who provide each other moral support, information, and advice on problems relating to some shared characteristic or experience: a support group for cancer survivors.[2]

2. A group of people with common experiences and concerns who provide emotional and moral support for one another.[3]

Support groups throughout recent decades include organizations like:

- MADD (Mothers Against Drunk Drivers)
- GriefShare (*for grieving the loss of a family member or friend*)
- Anger management groups
- Cancer support groups
- Parkinson's Disease support groups
- Adoption support groups
- AA (Alcoholics Anonymous)

- DivorceCare (*for Separated & Divorced*)
- Asthma Achievers
- Amputee Coalition of America
- Heart Association support groups
- Advanced breast cancer groups
- Homeschoolers Association groups
- Substance abuse support groups
- Abortion recovery support groups
- Widows and widowers groups
- Parenting support groups
- Domestic violence support groups
- Unemployment support groups
- Bankruptcy support groups
- Eating disorder groups (*for persons suffering from anorexia and bulimia.*)

This is just a partial listing of the thousands of support groups available to those who want to utilize the dynamics of a small group, which creates an environment where like-minded people can come together to share their thoughts, feelings, struggles, and successes concerning similar situations. Why so many? Because they *work*. They really help those who attend.

A Divorce Recovery Workshop publication[4] listed the most common benefits obtained by those who attended their support group settings. Those benefits add to the validity of support group activity being worthwhile and include:

* Enabling individuals to retake control of their present and future
* Functioning effectively again as a single person
* Helping restore self-esteem at a time when it is at its lowest

* Alleviating the tendency toward depression, isolation, and suicide
* Relieving tensions between partners to the benefit of children
* Reducing an individual's recovery period
* Enhancing personal development and growth

VARIOUS SUPPORT GROUPS

Support groups for those experiencing separation and divorce can be found throughout the country. There are many local churches that create their own unique plan for divorce ministry and do not utilize a pre-set program and curriculum. There are thousands of these around the country, and many of them will advertise on their local Christian radio, in a newspaper, or through other advertising outlets.

Another national program that churches have utilized, due to its Christian viewpoint or emphasis, is *Fresh Start*. They primarily put on weekend seminars.

> *"Fresh Start Seminars is a Christian ministry whose purpose is to touch the lives of the separated and divorced. We minister to both children and adults through seminars, support groups, books, and tapes."*

www.freshstartseminars.org

Some key points regarding Fresh Start are found on their website and include:

* Fresh Start seminars are held in local churches throughout North America. (The website has current postings of which states, cities, and

dates.) Typically the seminar is held over a Friday night and Saturday from 9:00 a.m. to about 5:00 p.m.

* Fresh Start then provides the church with materials to conduct a thirteen-week follow-up support group.
* Churches usually charge anywhere from $30-60 for the seminar, but the support groups are offered at no charge.
* Some churches also offer our Fresh Start for Kids program. This is also designed to run Friday night and Saturday.

My wife, Kathy, had a very positive experience with the workbooks and seminars of Fresh Start years after her divorce. She was a Facilitator during one of their weekend seminars at a local church where it was being held.

The other support group program Kathy got involved in was, of course, DivorceCare. Kathy eventually helped bring that support group ministry into her church soon after it first came out in 1996. Years later, it was where Kathy and I met as Leaders / Facilitators of that DivorceCare outreach.

There are many strong programs that we heartily recommend, such as those previously mentioned, but we feel that the following factors favoring DivorceCare are unmatched: its dual emphasis on both the separated and divorced (a powerful outreach for those in either phase), its accessibility (over 12,000 churches, in all fifty states and over twenty countries, nearly fifty-two weeks a year), its free cost (at times with a minor cost for a workbook), its join-anytime format, and its powerful use of videos and small groups.

Let's say you agree to visit a DivorceCare session while being separated. What do we suggest? First, it would be great for you to attend all thirteen weeks of the seminar. At an absolute minimum, we suggest you attend with the mindset that you'll try it out for at least three sessions no matter what, and then make another three-session commitment. Allowing enough time to be objective about your choice is important, because for many, any support group is a new experience, so you'll want to give yourself fair time to process it. Going only once can never bring the lasting impact we know can happen. You'll want to attend all thirteen sessions and glean what hundreds of thousands have discovered—a life-changing seminar!

The testimonies of those who have taken this step of attending a DivorceCare support group can hardly believe what great strength it gave them, and they strongly recommend others to jump at the chance to join one as soon as possible—whether one has been separated for days, months, or years.

"I was so unsure of what to do. I felt DivorceCare might help, but I was hesitant to show up in a group not knowing anyone else there. 'But I did just that when I took an aerobics class at our local health club,' I told myself. I didn't know a soul, but we were all there to lose weight, and it turned out great. So, even though it seemed hard to make the initial decision to attend my first DivorceCare meeting, I felt if I were to get emotionally stronger, faster, and for the sake of my kids I should 'just do it!' I am so glad I did! It was truly a warm and welcoming group that met me. And everyone

else was new to it, also! After a few weeks, I thought how much I had learned about separation and divorce and how practical and useful the insights were right now to get me through this properly. I strongly suggest others to 'just do it!' too."

Rhonda – Dallas, TX

"I was completely open to getting help, direction, and advice. I couldn't afford a professional counselor, so 'free' seminar had a nice sound to it. I have been helped far beyond what I ever thought possible! The videos, the small-group discussions, and the unity felt by all of us going through this together were incredible. My advice? Find a group and go. And keep going!"

Stan – Ft. Lauderdale, FL

When **Steve** got a phone call to attend a DivorceCare seminar from one of his closest friends, he jumped at the chance.

"When I got Mike's phone call, I was surfing the 'Net trying to find a used car. Mine was on its last breath, and I knew if I didn't find something soon I would be paying a small fortune in car repairs. I didn't need any more money problems; my attorney was plenty enough. Hanging up the phone I felt good about us finding a church that hosted DivorceCare. Mike and I had talked for weeks about going to one. We had a mutual friend from our community softball team that had gone to it, and he couldn't stop talking about it.

"Mike and I each had our own story, but bottom line is we were both in separation after nearly ten years of marriage. He left his wife but my wife left me, and we were both looking for help. His divorce

proceedings had started over a year earlier, but me and my wife were just recently apart. I only knew I didn't want to go through the emotional wreckage I saw Mike go through. He might be a little late for all this, but I felt really timely. Either way, I knew we both would get a lot out of this."

Steve – Albuquerque, NM

"Why was I there? The question came from the person sitting next to me at the start of another DivorceCare seminar session. 'Because I didn't come here the first time I was separated and eventually divorced!' His expression revealed he wanted me to continue, so I did. 'I really believe if I had come during my first marriage, when we were separated, I would not be here again after what is now my second separation in a second marriage!' Shaking his head slowly, I knew he got the point. 'I never thought I'd be separated from a second wife, but I am—but this time I'm taking action, determined to do my part to understand what to do now that I am.' With that said, the Group Leaders up front began an introduction. 'We'll talk afterwards,' I said, as my fellow attendee nodded in agreement. Later, we did just that!"

Barry – Seattle, WA

Now it's your turn! Go to **www.DivorceCare.org** or if you don't have easy access to the Internet, simply call 1-800-489-7778 (USA and Canada) to find the seminar group nearest you. Doing so will begin the steps to once again feeling a real sense of hope and direction.

Either way, my wife, Kathy, and I personally know the benefits of DivorceCare and know how incredibly helpful it can be at this crucial time in your life. No matter how long you've been separated—days, weeks, months, or years, even a *lot* of years—this seminar can help you.

We are praying that our words will encourage you in this decision to consider attending a support group, especially a DivorceCare nearest you.

But be it DivorceCare, Fresh Start, a local church Divorce Recovery Program of their own, or something else, we hope you don't fall into *Pitfall #1: "A support group? Not now, maybe later."* Instead, we hope you do it, and do it as soon as possible.

Next, we turn our attention to the opposite sex. It gets *very* interesting...

Scriptural Insights: Ch.1
A Support Group? Not Now, Maybe Later

Galatians 6:2 Bear one another's burdens, and so fulfill the law of Christ. **Proverbs 1:5** that the wise man may hear, and increase in learning; that the man of understanding may attain to sound counsel **Proverbs 19:20** Listen to counsel and receive instruction, that you may be wise in your latter end. **Proverbs 24:6** for by wise guidance you wage your war; and victory is in many advisors. **Proverbs 12:15** The way of a fool is right in his own eyes, but he who is wise listens to counsel. **2 Corinthians 1:3-4** Blessed be the God and Father of our Lord Jesus Christ, the Father of mercies and God of all comfort; **1:4** who comforts us in all our affliction, that we may be able to comfort those who are in any affliction, through the comfort with which we ourselves are comforted by God. **Proverbs 3:5-6** Trust in the LORD with all your heart, and don't lean on your own understanding. **3:6** In all your ways acknowledge him, and he will make your paths straight. **Proverbs 4:13** Take firm hold of instruction. Don't let her go. Keep her, for she is your life. **Proverbs 14:12** There is a way which seems right to a man, but in the end it leads to death. **Proverbs 15:22** Where there is no counsel, plans fail; but in a multitude of counselors they are established. **Proverbs 23:12** Apply your heart to instruction, and your ears to the words of knowledge. **Proverbs 13:20** One who walks with wise men grows wise, but a companion of fools suffers harm. **Ecclesiastes 4:9-10** Two are better than one, because they have a good reward for their labor. **4:10** For if they fall, the one will lift up his fellow; but woe to him who is alone when he falls, and doesn't have another to lift him up.

Pitfall 2

Opposite Sex Relationships— Yes, If They Help You!

I s it really best to experience a positive relationship (even a "friendship") with the opposite sex during this time of separation? Some of you believe this is not only OK but even needed—especially now, with all the pain and loss of love in your life.

For some of you reading this, the *last* thing you want is *anything* to do with the opposite sex—but it rarely lasts. Just wait and see. So, when you do start desiring the opposite sex again, we hope you take this next

Pitfall into serious consideration. It's one of the most powerful of the seven.

For those who are presently seeing someone at whatever level—full-fledged affair, early romantic stages, or just friends with the opposite sex—there are some suggestions to consider, especially from those who have gone on before you, those with real-life experiences of getting close to the opposite sex while in the marital separation phase. Some of their advice sounds like this:

> *"Stop it"..."Get out right now"..."You have no idea of the pain about to come into your life"..."It's soothing now, but the pain afterward is incredible"..."You think, 'you're different—this is special,' but it's a mirage that isn't real"..."If only I had listened to my friends warning me"..."Yes, it's OK to have relationships with the opposite sex—it's only a matter of when"...*

If you're like I was when I was separated, I would hear each one of those suggested words of advice, smile, and say, "Thanks, but that was your situation not mine; this is OK, and I know what I'm doing!" You see, I'm convinced that most of you reading this will simply ignore this advice and be like I was. But I figure if I only get through to a few of you, *even you*, then it will have been worth mentioning this *Pitfall #2*. Stay with me, OK?

The best illustration I've found to really apply to this situation is from Jim Talley of Oklahoma City[1] when he uses the example of you seeing someone with a broken foot. They take Novocain to kill the pain, and they continue to walk on it without first repairing and tending to the healing of their foot. They say they feel fine, but a friend comes by and points down at their foot and shows them the bone sticking out— chipped and broken. That's what a relationship with the opposite sex does. It's like Novocain, taking away the pain, but the problem is still there. You think it's helping, but in fact it's only helping your situation to become worse by the day. You're not *healing* first.

We've heard nearly every reason why a relationship with the opposite sex is OK or needed just now, especially during this time of separation:

> *"After all the rejection my soon-to-be ex gave me, it's great to be appreciated again!"*

> *"I haven't felt any sexual desire for so long since my marriage went downhill that to finally be sexually aroused again is too good to walk away from."*

> *"I'll show my soon-to-be ex that I still have what it takes to get someone!"*

> *"Love—just feeling love from someone is great, and to know it's mutual is sooo good!"*

> *"It's just talking, innocent talking. This person really listens and understands me—something my mate doesn't get!"*

> *"I'm as good as divorced, so why not date others? I've got to think about me for a change!"*

> *"We're just friends, really! There is nothing romantic or sexual about this. Just friends!"*

So what's *your* reason for having a relationship with the opposite sex while you're still married but in the separation phase? Whatever your reason, we're here to strongly suggest you reconsider your actions. Why? Let me give you *two* reasons to think about.

REASON #1: *MARRIED* - DON'T DATE

First, married people don't date! Sounds pretty basic, but that's because it is. Come on, how many people do you know who can honestly say, *"Sure, it's fine that a married person dates"*? Not many, if any, right? That's because we know what's basically right and wrong when it comes to being married. We even label that kind of behavior with words like *"affair"* or *"adultery"* or *"cheating"* or *"being unfaithful."* You get the idea.

And don't let the word *"dating"* throw you. You're seeing, spending time with, exchanging emotional and/or physical intimacy with another. We use the term "dating," but it means the same thing. Think of those phrases every time I use the word "date" or "dating" - *You're seeing, spending time with, exchanging emotional and/or physical intimacy with another.*

Whatever you do, please be honest with yourself. That's why we are sharing these important concepts with you. I know how much I denied calling my "friendships" with the opposite sex anything other than friendships. But as a married, even though *separated*, man, I was seeing, spending time with, and exchanging emotional and/or physical intimacy with another—in other words, dating. But I never called it that. Today I would, but back then, when I was hurting and disillusioned from my painful separation, I saw it as anything but dating, because I believed that married people don't date!

You probably believed that too, but that was back "then," when you weren't where you are now. You've changed since then, so now you believe that married people don't date, *unless…* Well, you fill in the blank.

The bottom line is, *not* dating when married is still the right thing to do, and we each know it. Dr. Jim Talley has conducted over 14,000 hours of marital counseling and gives his clients this simple quiz:[2]

The day **before** you get married, what are you? Single or Married? (*Single of course*)

The day **after** you get married, what are you? Single or Married? (*Married of course*)

The day **before** your divorce, what are you? Single or Married? (*Married*)

The day **after** your divorce, what are you? Single or Married? (*Single*)

And we all know it's *not* right for married people to be dating. You're still married. Doing what is *right* while still married, though not always easy, is still the right thing. You know it. We all know it.

Carlos struggled with that very issue during his separation.

> "*After three years of marriage and having been separated for over a year, I was starting to think differently about being open to dating. Over a quarter of my married life, I was separated! It was just the legal papers and negotiations that were holding things up now, and it might go on for another two months, my attorney told me! So I was open. Yes, I was still married, but…*"

"Well, that kind of thinking eventually allowed an opportunity to come my way. It just kind of happened. It started with friendly conversation among some of our mutual friends at a party one night, and before long, the talking became just with the two of us. Talking felt good and I sensed I was actually helping her with my thoughts on things. In the weeks that followed, we kept spending time together. I felt guilty at first, hoping no one would see us together, out like we were, but eventually I felt less guilty.

"But one night that changed. In my search for answers, in my desire to get this marriage over, my wife began to change. I mean really change. She wanted to talk; she wanted to reconsider what was going on. Now I was faced with what to do—stay unbending and continue this new-found relationship with the other person in my life, or break that off and be open to the one I had made wedding vows to? What a mess. My heart, once thought to be over all this, was now painfully torn open as I re-examined what was right and best for both of us—me and my wife."

Carlos – New York, NY

Teresa knew what was right, too. Here's her story.

"I was desperately lonely. Not at first, but after a few months of separation and once the routine of caring for the children by myself was firmly established, it started to show itself. The kids, the TV, the projects all started to really not fill the void anymore. I was lonely, and it wasn't going away. This was one of the very reasons I got married in the first place! I hated not having someone I cared for, a man in my life all the time. But here I was right back at that same situation, alone and lonely, without a companion.

"My friends suggested I start going out, even just with them on Fridays and Saturdays for a few drinks. They were single and definitely looking, if you know what I mean. But it didn't feel right to say 'yes,' since I was still married. But with their relentless reminders of what I was missing out on, I finally broke down and decided it was OK as long as I was going for the right reason—to be with my girlfriends—not looking for Mr. Right to end my loneliness.

"So there I was laughing, something I hadn't done in a long time. We even got up and danced. Seeing all four of us up on the floor was clearly an attention-getter for any normal, red-blooded guy.

"It was like the old days, when I knew it was just a matter of time that when the guys know you enjoy dancing but haven't done so with a guy yet, they just eventually start coming up and asking you to dance. Times had not changed. It wasn't long before I was asked, and, of course, I said 'no' but warmly suggested that any of my friends would love to dance! And so they did. Which only spurred other men to confidently walk over; knowing someone at our table would dance. But I held firm.

"Was it fun? Yes, but I knew I was married and until that was over, this type of lifestyle would be, too. I had no plans on returning despite the never-ending urging of my girlfriends. I was married."

Teresa – Boulder, CO

THE BOTTOM LINE

The bottom line about all this is that once you finalize your divorce, you *are* single—again. Being single means you can date. It's perfectly right to. The question will no longer be "*Can* you date," but rather becomes an issue of *when*.

Yet, just when you get the green light (to date), we suggest you allow it to turn into a yellow caution, then a red light! "*You've got to be kidding me*," you say. Well, no. But that's for another time, another book. Yet if you do want to know a few initial reasons for you to go slow—if not stop dating altogether—for a season just after legally being divorced, here are a few:

1) Establish dating guidelines for yourself.
2) Become stable and whole.

Before dating, you'll want to take the time to establish dating guidelines for yourself and be sure you are not dating in order to fill a void, cover a pain, or for a thousand other wrong reasons. You're still in need of a time of healing, of stabilizing. You want to be healed and whole, finally seeing someone else who's healed and whole so you two can enjoy each other, not try to use the other to fix your hurts, pain, and other messed up areas. Taking these two practical steps is worth the wait.

> *"Did I wait to date until I was legally divorced and no longer technically married? Oh yeah, I waited. Waited about six hours. I held on for all those years, not wanting to send myself or my kids a wrong message. But the day of my divorce, I had agreed to go out with this guy for that night. And what a disaster!*
>
> *After fifteen years of marriage, I was so not ready for the dating scene, not ready for the very process of going out. I felt awkward and found myself in compromising situations I couldn't believe I allowed*

myself into. That night I was going places and doing things I never would have imagined. Nothing serious ultimately happened but could have. I clearly had lost touch with the dating scene, and needed to re-establish some new guidelines for myself and my dates. Especially since the dating scene had drastically changed from when I was last in it. A lot had changed, and it was a world I had to be prepared for and not just jump into.

"Also, I was not ready personally. I had a lot of healing to do and knew that night this kind of stuff was not going to help me gain stability. I needed some time, divorced but healing, by myself. Years later, after many dates along the way, when healing came and I became stable and whole, I met another man who was healed and whole over his divorce. Yes, we dated. Better still, yes, we married!"

Kathy Fallon – Florida
Co-Author of Separated But
Not Divorced

So dating, even *after* a divorce, should be approached slowly and with caution. My wife, **Kathy**, learned that lesson.

Now, back to our main topic for this Chapter 2: *Opposite-sex relationships while in marital separation.* As you recall, we said you should reconsider your interest in the opposite sex during the separation phase because: First, married people don't date (*seeing, spending time with, exchanging emotional and/or physical intimacy with another*). Second, you need to stabilize. Sounds like a common theme, doesn't it? That's because it's so fundamental to making better choices on this road of separation (and divorce).

REASON #2 – YOU NEED TO STABALIZE

Studies[3] have shown that the top ten situations that are the most stressful in one's life include the following:
1) Death of a spouse
2) Marital divorce
3) Marital separation

Do you realize you've made it into the *top three* of the Top Ten List of the Most Stressful Situations? Research is very clear about this, that seriously stressful situations have major impacts on one's life: physical impact, emotional impact, mental impact, financial impact, social impact, work function impact, spiritual impact—and the list goes on. Attention has to be given to such areas when serious stress is reached. Marital separation *is* impacting you, whether you think so or not, and any denial of such only makes it harder for you to begin working out a stabilization plan of healing and wholeness.

Relationships with the opposite sex at this stressful time are **not** the recommendation of skilled counselors, wise ministers, and thousands of those who have gone before you on this road of separation. What they *do* recommend as practical suggestions for refraining from opposite sex relations (for a season) are the following:

Suggestion #1: Avoid locations where singles are looking for singles. This includes places like bars, Internet dating websites or chat-rooms for singles, even local church singles functions like Bible studies, fellowships, or retreats.

Suggestion #2: Begin to develop or strengthen same-sex relationships. This is usually easier for women than for men, but the effort has been truly rewarding for those who commit to doing so. Pray for guidance, and seek out same-sex Christian friends, attend same-sex Bible studies, attend same-sex retreats and conferences. Attending or participating in sports events with a same-sex friend might be the choice of some. It's what you uniquely need just now—not forever—to replace the opposite sex.

Suggestion #3: Attend co-ed support groups without dating in mind. This is the only context we suggest, apart from regular church worship and normal employment, that you engage with the opposite sex for this unique period in your life. You're still married, but, of course, getting their perspectives within a co-ed support group is great.

These three simple but straightforward suggestions can help ease the "need" for opposite-sex relations, which is a normal, healthy thing to want—just not now, while separated. Instead, focus on *you* right now, in order for *you* to become healed and whole. Really strive for personal stabilization. This needs to be a *major* priority. A priority that **James** came to embrace.

> *"When the reality of our situation began to sink in and I knew separation was the only thing left to do, I had no idea what was ahead of me. The night I moved out, I experienced such rejection and loneliness, but it was only the beginning of a long journey. The legal hassles, the lies and half-truths being stated about me made me sick. I felt revengeful and angry. Hurt and disillusioned. Empty and depressed.*

> *"Like being stunned but eventually coming back to reality, I realized how badly I needed some real help.*

Not help to fix our marriage; it seemed much too late for that. Rather, help for me to gain custody of myself again, to not be so out of control with my emotions, my thoughts, my everything! I determined to focus on me. Not that I wasn't open to seeing her change, too, but my focus started shifting more toward me gaining wholeness, becoming healed. That one decision is really what started my turn-around. Yes, the other stuff was still out there—the legal issues, the fighting, the battle over the kids and money—but my focus was on me. It's what saved me.

"Looking back, I see that even more. We eventually got the divorce. She eventually married someone else. But within me I'm whole, healed, and free from guilt. That's not true with her. I wish it were, but even she is vocal about how bitter and angry she still is, as when she first left me. I can see now how she never discovered the importance of finding healing and wholeness. She's carried all that pain and baggage into her second marriage, and the strain of it has had a visible impact on that relationship.

"I strongly suggest staying focused on yourself for a while, until you know you're healed."

James – San Diego, CA

Veronica became aware of self-focus, for healing and wholeness, from the example of a close friend. Here's her story:

"When I saw one of my close friends go through her divorce, I made a commitment I wouldn't do what I saw her do. She practically self-destructed before my eyes. After her husband had cheated on her for the umpteenth time, she had it. She filed for divorce, and in her head this marriage was over—though in a

very real sense it had been over for years, since she was emotionally dead to him over the last three years. Their sexless, non-communicative marriage was only the shell of one. Now she knew it was soon to be legally over, too.

"But what I saw her do surprised most everyone. She went off the deep end big time. The very thing she hated about her husband—sleeping around—she was doing while still in the throes of separation. She was on a pendulum swing, and it was going higher. It wasn't just me; all her friends couldn't believe what they were watching her do!

"So when I came into my separation, I just determined I was not going that way. Something better had to be waiting for me instead of an endless search to rid the pain by going to extremes.

"I saw this as a window of opportunity to re-examine myself, to ask some tough questions about what I wanted and where was I going. Like a personal retreat, I took any extra free time to really get to know myself better—something I had clearly not done during nine years of marriage. It was all about my husband and the kids. No time for me, a total loss of balance. I had let it happen then, but I was determined not to let it happen again. So far it hasn't, and I know that I know I'm a better person for it. Someday, someone will be glad I found a new me, a stronger me, a healed and whole me."

Veronica – Boston, MA

The opposite sex: it's not a question of you *ever* connecting with them again. It's an issue of *when* and an issue of *who you are* at the time. Married or single?

Healed or hurting? You will know the answers to those issues if you're really honest with yourself.

Congratulations on completing *Pitfalls #1 and #2*! We trust you are still planning to stay with us as we examine the rest. We hope you continue approaching each *Pitfall* with the mindset of: "*I may or may not agree with this, but I'll consider it.*"

Pitfall #3 is coming next. Are you already in this *Pitfall* and don't even see it? The details may surprise you.

Scriptural Insights: Ch.2
Opposite Sex Relationships—Yes, if They Help You!

Proverbs 3:5-5 Trust in the LORD with all your heart, and don't lean on your own understanding. **3:6** In all your ways acknowledge him, and he will make your paths straight. **Proverbs 5:3-13** For the lips of an adulteress drip honey. Her mouth is smoother than oil, **5:4** But in the end she is as bitter as wormwood, and as sharp as a two-edged sword. **5:5** Her feet go down to death. Her steps lead straight to Sheol. **5:6** She gives no thought to the way of life. Her ways are crooked, and she doesn't know it. **5:7** Now therefore, my sons, listen to me. Don't depart from the words of my mouth. **5:8** Remove your way far from her. Don't come near the door of her house, **5:9** lest you give your honor to others, and your years to the cruel one; **5:10** lest strangers feast on your wealth, and your labors enrich another man's house. **5:11** You will groan at your latter end, when your flesh and your body are consumed, **5:12** and say, "How I have hated instruction, and my heart despised reproof; **5:13** neither have I obeyed the voice of my teachers, nor turned my ear to those who instructed me! **Proverbs 6:32** He who commits adultery with a woman is void of understanding. He who does it destroys his own soul. **Exodus 20:14** "You shall not commit adultery. **2 Corinthians 6:14** Don't be unequally yoked with unbelievers, for what fellowship have righteousness and iniquity? Or what fellowship has light with darkness? **1 Thessalonians 4:3** For this is the will of God: your sanctification, that you abstain from sexual immorality,

4:4 that each one of you know how to possess himself of his own vessel in sanctification and honor, **Hebrews 13:4** Let marriage be held in honor among all, and let the bed be undefiled: but God will judge the sexually immoral and adulterers. **Matthew 5:27** "You have heard that it was said, 'You shall not commit adultery;' **5:28** but I tell you that everyone who gazes at a woman to lust after her has committed adultery with her already in his heart. **1 Corinthians 6:13-20** "Foods for the belly, and the belly for foods," but God will bring to nothing both it and them. But the body is not for sexual immorality, but for the Lord; and the Lord for the body. **6:14** Now God raised up the Lord, and will also raise us up by his power. **6:15** Don't you know that your bodies are members of Christ? Shall I then take the members of Christ, and make them members of a prostitute? May it never be! **6:16** Or don't you know that he who is joined to a prostitute is one body? For, "The two," says he, "will become one flesh." **6:17** But he who is joined to the Lord is one spirit. **6:18** Flee sexual immorality! "Every sin that a man does is outside the body," but he who commits sexual immorality sins against his own body. **6:19** Or don't you know that your body is a temple of the Holy Spirit which is in you, which you have from God? You are not your own, **6:20** for you were bought with a price. Therefore glorify God in your body and in your spirit, which are God's. **2 Timothy 2:22** Flee from youthful lusts; but pursue righteousness, faith, love, and peace with those who call on the Lord out of a pure heart. **1 Corinthians 10:13** No temptation has taken you except what is common to man. God is faithful, who will not allow you to be tempted above what you are able, but will with the temptation also make the way of escape, that you may be able to endure it. **Proverbs 25:28** Like a city that is broken down and without walls is a man whose spirit is without restraint. **1 Peter 1:13-16** Therefore, prepare your minds for action, be sober and set your hope fully on the grace that will be brought to you at the revelation of Jesus Christ **1:14** as children of obedience, not conforming yourselves according to your former lusts as in your ignorance, **1:15** but just as he who called you is holy, you yourselves also be holy in all of your behavior; **1:16** because it is written, "You shall be holy; for I am holy." **Revelations 21:8** But for the cowardly, unbelieving, sinners, abominable, murderers, sexually immoral, sorcerers, idolaters, and all liars, their part is in the lake that burns with fire and sulfur, which is the second death." **2 Peter 1:5-6** Yes, and for this very cause adding on your part all diligence, in your faith supply moral excellence; and in moral excellence, knowledge; **1:6** and in knowledge, self-control; and in self-control patience; and in patience godliness; **Romans 6:12-13** Therefore don't let sin reign in your mortal body, that you should obey it in its lusts. **6:13** Neither present your members to sin as instruments of unrighteousness, but present yourselves to God, as alive from the dead, and your members as instruments of righteousness to God. **Romans 8:5** For those who live according to the flesh set their minds on the things of the flesh, but those who live according to the Spirit, the things of the Spirit. **Romans 12:1-2** Therefore I urge you, brothers, by the mercies of God, to present your bodies a living sacrifice, holy, acceptable to God, which is your spiritual service. **12:2** Don't be conformed to this world, but be transformed by the renewing of your mind, so that you may prove what is the good, well-pleasing, and perfect will of God. **Galatians 5:16-21** But I say, walk by the Spirit, and you won't fulfill the lust of the flesh. **5:17** For the flesh lusts against the Spirit, and the Spirit against the flesh; and these are contrary to one another, that you may not do the things that you desire. **5:18** But if you are led by the Spirit, you are not under the law. **5:19** Now the works of the flesh are obvious, which are: adultery, sexual immorality, uncleanness, lustfulness, **5:20** idolatry, sorcery, hatred, strife, jealousies, outbursts of anger, rivalries, divisions, heresies, **5:21** envyings, murders, drunkenness, orgies, and things like these; of which I forewarn you, even as I also forewarned you, that those who practice such things will not inherit the Kingdom of God. **Colossians 3:5-6** Put to death therefore your members which are on the earth: sexual immorality, uncleanness, depraved passion, evil desire, and covetousness, which is idolatry; **3:6** for which things' sake the wrath of God comes on the children of disobedience. **Titus 2:11-12** For the grace of God has appeared, bringing salvation to all men, **2:12** instructing us to the intent that, denying ungodliness and worldly lusts, we would live soberly, righteously, and godly in this present world **James 1:13-15** Let no man say when he is tempted, "I am tempted by God," for God can't be tempted by evil, and he himself tempts no one. **1:14** But each one is tempted, when he is drawn away by his own lust, and enticed. **1:15** Then the lust, when it has conceived, bears sin; and the sin, when it is full grown, brings forth death.

Pitfall

Making Major Decisions *Before* Gaining Objectivity

This is a classic *Pitfall*, because emotions are running at full throttle while reason seems to be back in the pit-stop, completely off the race track. It's a time for balance and objectivity, which primarily will come through **time, input from experienced people, and information gathered from varied resources.**

Separation is *not* conducive to balance or objectivity. Emotions seem to rule, and reason seems to be nowhere. How do we let that happen? It's a great question, but there's no easy answer. We only know that it *does* happen, even to the most intellectually wise people who are fully in control of their decisions. Something very powerful happens when one goes through marital separation, and it really doesn't help the major decision-making process at that time. Often it's because of our emotional state that we end up making these major decisions in the first place. But for whatever reason, making *major* decisions while in marital separation is potentially disastrous.

Consider these: Quitting a job or choosing a new one. Selling a house or buying a new one. Going on an expensive vacation. Buying any new major item like cars, jewelry, furniture, clothes—possibly in large volumes. Cashing in on retirement funds, investments, or real estate holdings. Or just the popular choice of running up your credit cards to the max on anything and everything at $5, $10, $50, $100 at a time until thousands of dollars have been credited and you're now opening new credit card accounts to continue the process. Spending $95, $120, $150 an hour on attorney fees to get this divorce over as quickly as possible. To decide to give in on every legal demand—you just want out of this marriage—or choosing to fight for everything—how dare he or she thinks you'll let them have that; they deserve nothing! The very choice to divorce instead of attempting another chance at reconciliation. The choice to divorce as quickly as possible. The choice to divorce at all.

These are all *major* decisions that we find ourselves in when we enter this separation phase. It's a road we travel depleted of balance and objectivity. The onslaught of our emotions has drained us, and now is *not* the time for these major decisions to be made.

Even if, in the end, much later down the road than now, we still make decisions in each of these areas, they can be made with balance and objectivity, the outcome being better, wiser, healthier decisions for not only ourselves but for all who are impacted by them.

"I was in such a hurry to end this marriage. Once we decided to separate, that was the starting line for me, and I was going to get to the finish line fast and first. First to secure an attorney, then to selling every non-essential I could—like my boat to the camper— before she could get her hands on them. My financial needs started to pile up quickly. I was full throttle.

"Almost immediately I was paying for another apartment in addition to our present house. I was paying for attorney fees that were skyrocketing out of sight. Just simple phone calls and emails were costing me a small fortune at $175/hour. I couldn't push it fast enough, and every delay tactic on her attorney's side was again costing me more money. I sold off stock, real estate, and drained a lot of my savings.

"Fast, furious, and foolish - that's what it was and I was. I shake my head just thinking about those times. I had lost all sense of clarity or better judgment. I was hurting inside, and I just thought, 'Do whatever it takes to get this over, and the pain will then go away.' It was that very belief that caused me even more pain. Had I chosen to step back and slow down and get a fix on what was going on, I would have made a thousand better choices. Not only for me, but for my kids, too.

"It wasn't just about material things. Emotionally and relationally they lost out—we lost out as parent to child—because I was in a hurry. Remember, I was the guy who was going to get to the finish line fast and first. It was one race I wish I hadn't won."

Anthony – Jersey City, NJ

TIME

Time, just *time*, will become a great safeguard in obtaining balance and objectivity, even though it's one thing that seems impossible to control. Well, ancient's said that about the wind, too. No, we can't stop the wind, but we can and have *used* it to sail the vast oceans of the world, even to discover new ones! The same goes for time. We can't stop time from moving on, like the saying goes, "Time waits for no man,", but you can use it to bring distance to observe things with greater clarity. You can choose *not* to make certain decisions as time keeps moving.

We strongly suggest you buy yourself more *time*, somehow, some way, before making major decisions in this separation phase. Not only does it allow reason to come back on track, but emotions have a better chance to once again be properly placed in the scheme of things. Yes, with time, major decisions will be made, but with balance and objectivity alongside it. We've often counseled others by saying, "Whatever you're deciding, just go about it *slower*." Slower is always better—even if you don't think so.

"Feelings? Love? Those had left me years ago. As a new bride over seventeen years earlier, I remember the excitement of finding just the right romantic card in the card shop to express my deep emotions for him. Reading those creatively written messages with the words 'Love' and 'Affection' on them so conveyed what I felt for him. But buying cards over the last two years was a chore, a difficult task of by-passing each and every card that had the word 'Love' on it, for I so didn't feel love and he knew it. I felt nothing. No love, no concern, no hate, no anger, just deadness. Just

emptiness—a far cry from that joyful simplistic bliss I once knew and cherished, never in a million years thinking it would leave me. Yet it did. Slowly but surely.

"Cards with those full-cover photos and blank inside were my salvation. I'd buy one of those and jot a few words of 'Happy Birthday' or 'Merry Christmas' or 'Happy Father's Day,' or whatever the occasion called for. Just avoiding any cards declaring words of emotions from 'Your loving wife.' I did it mostly for the kids, for them to see that Mom always gave Dad a card. But he knew the situation only too well.

"When he finally moved out, determined he'd had enough of my 'deadness' from the relationship, I was hardly in a position to stop him or even suggest alternatives. But after months of him out of the house, out of my life, something started to happen. I started to reflect more, to think more about what was important. About what we had built for seventeen years, even if the last two were 'dry, dead, and meaningless.' Having time to myself caused me to want more time. I was experiencing something, and I didn't want to be rushed. So I stalled things. I stalled his suggestions of making this permanent by getting a divorce. I slowed up any part of the process that was forcing me to plunge ahead and finish off our marriage.

"He couldn't believe I was taking my time, especially when I had showed no resistance to him at the start of our separation. But now I was seeing and feeling things differently. Could it be that is all I needed? We needed? Time to step back? To get a more balanced perspective?

We're still in the process. Still separated—but slowed down to nearly a halt. It's giving us both time for a new perspective."

Gina – Greensboro, NC

INPUT FROM "EXPERIENCED" PEOPLE

Another advantage to added time during this separation phase is that it will allow you to receive input from *"experienced"* people and gather information from varied resources.

The goal, of course, is to make major decisions with balance and objectivity. Hearing and learning what others have done during their times of separation can help achieve that goal. You will learn what things they *regretted* doing while separated and things they feel they did *right* and would encourage others to consider doing.

We're talking about getting *input from experienced people*, those who have gone through separation, have gone through divorce. It's amazing to me how many of my friends, relatives, and co-workers had tons of advice for me even though they had never been separated or divorced. Can you think of a few in your life? I hear you right now saying, *"Can I? Let the list begin!"* We're not talking about lack of sincerity or lack of strong convictions on their part. For the most part, they are simply, sincerely *wrong* about most of the advice they give you, just like they gave me. And those that *did* go through separation and divorce might have no clue about what they should have done differently, because they were so messed up themselves that the "advice" they are giving you is their autobiography, not good advice! So where can we go for good advice?

We suggest you go to those who are healed and whole, those who have traveled the road of separation and have learned from it. People like that can be found in *DivorceCare* -type ministry seminars and in friends you know who have wisely learned and are no longer bitter.

"The first time I met John and Carol was at church, during my first DivorceCare meeting. They were at the registration table along with a few other smiling faces warmly welcoming me and others to the start of a new class. Later that night, after the seminar was over, I walked up to Carol to ask her advice about an 'issue' I was struggling with—my husband! Specifically, it was about him calling me, and it becoming really emotional for me.

"She was so approachable, so caring, so understanding. Knowing she, too, had experienced separation made me even more receptive to her advice. When we got into the issue, she asked some questions, and then gave me some incredibly practical advice—and it worked! A technique she had learned over the years working with those separated and divorced. It wasn't the last time I sought her guidance, either. But that night, I learned what to do when my husband calls on the phone and it starts getting heated. Thanks to Carol!"

Vanessa – Homestead, FL

"I knew Steve from the company I had been with for over ten years. We had worked on the same floor for years and over that period had connected up a bunch of times. We had other mutual office friends, and we all would go out from time to time to events or just for lunch. We were pretty shocked when word of his divorce made its way through the office gossip mill. He had some rough months, and we all knew why. I never really talked to him about it. Never needed to and felt it was his private life. Who was I to ask questions?

"But when my wife and I separated, he was the first person I thought of who I knew would understand. I didn't approach him, but he did me one morning

while everyone was invading some fresh donuts someone brought and placed near the coffee maker. I was going back for a second helping when he was grabbing another coffee refill. 'How's it going?' he asked while adding some sugar to his brew. 'Not the best,' I said, 'I'm sure you've heard.' Sipping slowly he looked up and said, 'Yeah, I'm really sorry about your marriage.' I knew his concern was real, both by his tone and body language, but mostly because I knew he could relate. He didn't probe but added, 'If I let you borrow a book that gave me some great advice during my divorce, would you give it back to me?' he said with a smirk, trying to lighten the mood yet be of help. 'Sure!' I said, without a moment's hesitation. 'Great, I'll dig it out and drop it by your desk tomorrow morning. It's a great read and really helped me out. And if you want to talk about any of it while you're plowing through it, I'd be glad to,' he said, as he walked toward the hallway. 'Thanks for the offer,' I said and smiled with appreciation as he began turning the corner toward his office.

"That simple encounter was the start of many future conversations over coffee. He's been a real help with his insights and personal example of how to get through a divorce and be sane enough to talk about it! I only hope I can be that for someone one day. But for now, the focus is on me. By the way, the book was a great read!"

Warren – Washington, DC

<u>INFORMATION FROM RESOURCES</u>

Other great varied resources are books, magazine articles, audio and videos, and internet websites. These are usually produced by people outside your geographical area. You are therefore most likely *not* going to be able to talk to these people in person, but you can learn from their experiences and knowledge as expressed in their handiwork.

> *"During my time of separation, I turned to books I found on the subject. Author after author shared some really good insights. Each had personally experienced separation and divorce, so they spoke from experience and research they gleaned from others. One book talked about emotional stages one experiences when going through this phase, and the way he described it helped me to see where I was, where my kids were. It was like I had been talking to him myself, because the way he described each of the five stages was so accurate and personal—so me!"*
>
> **Janet – Aniston, AL**

> *"After some initial searching on the internet, I found a website with a lot of CDs and books. I ordered a few CDs and listened to them in my car each day driving to and from work. Man, what a difference they made in me by helping me better understand what I was going through! I thought this was just me experiencing some of this stuff, these feelings, these problems, with my pending divorce. We still have a few weeks before it's finalized, but the practical things I've applied over the last three months have really helped.*
>
> *I remember asking a friend of mine who went through a divorce if he had any books or tapes he could loan me. Not a single one! He never heard of any during his entire divorce. That's what got me looking in the first place. He could have really used them, but try telling him that!"*
>
> **Ernie – Charlotte, NC**

As with the support groups mentioned in Chapter One, so it is true with *resources*. There are many out there, some offering good "secular" advice, but finding ones with Christian authors is worth the effort. The advice from such authors provides both experience and a Christian perspective—a biblical position. We strongly recommend you begin with these types of resources first. You can find some excellent books and tapes like this on the **www.DivorceCare.org** website under their Bookstore section. Another Christian website for books is our own **www.SocietyD.com**, which has many books relating to issues of importance for those going through separation or divorce. Once there, go to the Word Search function and put in the word: ***Divorce.***

We'd also recommend **www.TroubledWith.com**, which is actually a ministry of Dr. James Dobson's Focus on the Family. On the website, under the Relationships column, is the category of Separation. It offers articles and books on the issue. They also have other great web pages of content, on their homepage, dealing with issues of interest for those on this road of separation. So, you'll want to check many of them out. *TroubledWith.com* is well worth your time to view all the titles and subjects. These websites are only a few key strokes away!

(*Word of caution: Because websites are constantly being changed or eliminated, we suggest you do additional searches using any main search engine such as Google.*)

Your local Christian bookstore might also offer a few books on separation and divorce, but we haven't found anything nearly as extensive as on the websites we're mentioning. Regular local bookstores like Barnes &

Noble, Waldenbooks, and Borders also seem to have very few Christian authors on these issues sitting on their bookshelves. But, all do special ordering if requested.

Note of Observation: As my wife, Kathy, and I have read and reviewed many books over the years, we have concluded that there are fewer resources for those in the *separation phase* than any other.

You'll find quite a bit on dating and engagement to be married. There are enormous amounts of information for improving and strengthening marriages. You will find an extensive amount for those who have actually gone through divorce and a growing number of books on re-marriage. But between marriage and divorce, that time of *separation*, you find very, very little. What many who are separated have done is find areas that can be applied from those other categories, even if not written exclusively for those who are separated—for example, books that deal with issues on emotions, forgiveness, depression, loneliness, anger, sex, finances, children, communication, legal issues, and much more. So even if books are written for those in the marriage, engagement, re-marriage, or even the divorced phases, they are still beneficial to those in a "*separation only*" phase.

Our point is, seek out information from varied resources, but be aware that a lot of the advice will come in books not explicitly written for those only in the separation phase.

BALANCE & OBJECTIVITY DO COME

Balance and objectivity will come through *time, input from experienced people, and information from other resources*. What do you need to do to ensure that these become a part of your life right now? It might not be easy, especially if you're in the midst of making major decisions right now—today, or tomorrow, even yesterday or the recent past—but you *can* begin to slow the process down. You *can* take steps to hear from experienced others in person or seek out other resources. This is all about choices. You *can* do this. Kathy and I wish we had; that's why we urge you to do so. It's all about gaining balance and objectivity *before* making those major decisions.

That's it for *Pitfall #3*. The next chapter, *Pitfall # 4*, is one well worth, knowing, because you have or will soon have certain "*symptoms*." Ignoring them, not knowing or understanding them, isn't what you need right now.

Scriptural Insights: Ch.3
Making Major Decisions *Before* Gaining Objectivity

Ecclesiastes 3:1 For everything there is a season, and a time for every purpose under heaven **Ecclesiastes 8:5** Whoever keeps the commandment shall not come to harm, and his wise heart will know the time and procedure. **Genesis 49:18** I have waited for your salvation, LORD. **Psalm 27:14** Wait for the LORD. Be strong, and let your heart take courage. Yes, wait for the LORD. **Psalm 33:20** Our soul has waited for the LORD. He is our help and our shield. **Psalm 37:7** Rest in the LORD, and wait patiently for him. Don't fret because of him who prospers in his way, because of the man who makes wicked plots happen. **Psalm 40:1** I waited patiently for the LORD. He turned to me, and heard my cry. **Psalm 69:3** I am weary with my crying. My throat is dry. My eyes fail, looking for my God. **Proverbs 20:22** Don't say, "I will pay back evil." Wait for the LORD, and he will save you. **Lamentations 3:25** The LORD is good to those who wait for him, to the soul that seeks him. **Proverbs 4:5-8** Get wisdom. Get understanding. Don't forget, neither swerve from the words of my mouth. **4:6** Don't forsake her, and she will preserve you. Love her, and she will keep you. **4:7**

Wisdom is supreme. Get wisdom. Yes, though it costs all your possessions, get understanding. **4:8** Esteem her, and she will exalt you. She will bring you to honor, when you embrace her. **Proverbs 4:13** Take firm hold of instruction. Don't let her go. Keep her, for she is your life. **James 6:12** Do you see a man wise in his own eyes? There is more hope for a fool than for him. **Psalm 32:8** I will instruct you and teach you in the way which you shall go. I will counsel you with my eye on you. **Proverbs 3:5-6** Trust in the LORD with all your heart, and don't lean on your own understanding. **3:6** In all your ways acknowledge him, and he will make your paths straight. **Isaiah 42:16** I will bring the blind by a way that they don't know. I will lead them in paths that they don't know. I will make darkness light before them, and crooked places straight. I will do these things, and I will not forsake them. **John 16:13a** However when he, the Spirit of truth, has come, he will guide you into all truth. **Romans 12:2** Don't be conformed to this world, but be transformed by the renewing of your mind, so that you may prove what is the good, well-pleasing, and perfect will of God. **1:5** But if any of you lacks wisdom, let him ask of God, who gives to all liberally and without reproach; and it will be given to him. **Deuteronomy 31:8** The LORD, he it is who does go before you; he will be with you, he will not fail you, neither forsake you: don't be afraid, neither be dismayed." **Philippians 4:6-7** In nothing be anxious, but in everything, by prayer and petition with thanksgiving, let your requests be made known to God. **4:7** And the peace of God, which surpasses all understanding, will guard your hearts and your thoughts in Christ Jesus. **Proverbs 13:20** One who walks with wise men grows wise, but a companion of fools suffers harm. **Proverbs 27:9** Perfume and incense bring joy to the heart; so does earnest counsel from a man's friend. **Ecclesiastes 4:9-10** Two are better than one, because they have a good reward for their labor. **4:10** For if they fall, the one will lift up his fellow; but woe to him who is alone when he falls, and doesn't have another to lift him up. **Proverbs 3:13-4** Happy is the man who finds wisdom, the man who gets understanding. **3:14** For her good profit is better than getting silver, and her return is better than fine gold. **Proverbs 12:17-18** He who is truthful testifies honestly, but a false witness lies. **12:18** There is one who speaks rashly like the piercing of a sword, but the tongue of the wise heals. **Proverbs 16:16** How much better it is to get wisdom than gold! Yes, to get understanding is to be chosen rather than silver. **Job 12:12-13** With aged men is wisdom, in length of days understanding. **12:13** "With God is wisdom and might. He has counsel and understanding. **Psalm 37:30**

The mouth of the righteous talks of wisdom. His tongue speaks justice. **Psalm 111:10** The fear of the LORD is the beginning of wisdom. All those who do his work have a good understanding. **Proverbs 1:7** The fear of the LORD is the beginning of knowledge; but the foolish despise wisdom and instruction. **Proverbs 12:1** Whoever loves correction loves knowledge, but he who hates reproof is stupid. **Proverbs 14:12** There is a way which seems right to a man, but in the end it leads to death. **Proverbs 14:15** A simple man believes everything, but the prudent man carefully considers his ways. **Proverbs 15:7a** The lips of the wise spread knowledge **Proverbs 24:14** So you shall know wisdom to be to your soul; if you have found it, then there will be a reward, your hope will not be cut off. **Proverbs 19:27** If you stop listening to instruction, my son, you will stray from the words of knowledge. **Proverbs 18:2** A fool has no delight in understanding, but only in revealing his own opinion. **Proverbs 18:15** The heart of the discerning gets knowledge. The ear of the wise seeks knowledge.

SocietyD.com
When You
Separate or Divorce

Pitfall 4

* * *

Separation Symptoms? Not Aware of Any!

The year was 1981. He was always known for his endless energy and his party lifestyle. A trendy jet-setter, his life was fast paced with international friends and lovers. Though he sometimes pushed his body to the edge with sleepless nights and drug use, he always bounced back ready for more. This time was different. His energy wasn't coming back like before. His flu-like symptoms weren't leaving.

A doctor's visit proved negative for mono or hepatitis, but more testing was ordered. Then other symptoms came forward: the loss of appetite, the aches, pains, and weight loss. Different doctors, different tests—all proved fruitless in understanding what he was experiencing. The typical answers for the known symptoms were not working. As the months passed he would improve, only to find himself in another relapse. But time was not on his side.

He rapidly saw the rare disease, or whatever it was, take over at alarming speed, creating a frail skeleton, his skin layered with sores and tortured by pain that could not be eased. Then he died. Not knowing the cause, the doctors could not treat it. He would become known as Patient Zero.[1] He was one of the first of tens of millions. He had AIDS.

This is a serious example of having something and not knowing what's going on. Since then, we and the world have spent billions of dollars to understand the disease, educating others about it, slowing it down, with hopes of one day eliminating it.

So whether it's the common cold or AIDS, measles or mumps, a tumor or a belly ache, they each have unique characteristics, symptoms, stages that can be felt, seen, and understood.

You might say, "Hey I don't have a disease, I'm just getting a legal divorce." Maybe not, but what might have started out as a legal proceeding is and will become so much more than that. You will experience a trauma of sorts, a stress-related experience that will affect you in varying degrees. That's why divorce and separation are #2 and #3 of the most stressful of life experiences.[2] When we are married, we are bonded emotionally and spiritually in *oneness*; when divided, it is not a clean break but a jagged tearing of one becoming two. The stages and characteristics of this tearing are well documented, understood, and treatable.

You are experiencing or soon will begin to experience these phenomena, and if you're not aware of them, that they are normal and expected, you will think something is wrong with you or won't be able to figure out what's wrong. Knowing these symptoms and what to do about them is incredibly healing. That's worth repeating: *Knowing these symptoms and what to do about them is incredibly healing.*

> *"I thought I was going crazy! Out of nowhere I would begin crying. I was so moody, and it wasn't even that time of the month! I was forgetting things, my concentration was short lived. Everything I tried to do to fix it wasn't working."*
>
> ### Beth – Louisville, KY

> *"One thing I was not known for was my anger. Honestly! If anything, I held stuff in, but I never expressed it outwardly. Whatever I did feel inside, it was minimal. I rarely got upset over anything. Then it started. Feelings of anger like I had never known before. Raw, deep, painful feelings that became fuel for anger that I didn't know I could experience. Then my thoughts of revenge clouded my thinking. Plotting ways to get back at her and how my anger just fed more destructive thoughts. If it weren't for my kids and the Christian reputation I had at my church, I would have probably acted out those stupid revengeful thoughts. How long would this last? Was this a new me—now showing so much anger? I was a mess."*
>
> ### Phillip – Washington, DC

The reality is that there *are* some identifiable symptoms those in separation *will* experience. When you see them you might think you know what they fully mean, but that's usually not the case. The *words* you know, but the way they express themselves is something far greater. Which "words" have you experienced since your separation? Did you put a name on what you were experiencing or just group it into one big *"Oh I'm just going through divorce stuff, so I feel this way"* category? Trust us; you can be much more specific than that. Once you are, you can also treat and work through that specific feeling much more effectively. Here are just a handful of "words." Which ones have you experienced?

* Anger
* Depression
* Loneliness
* Unforgiveness

As I've already mentioned, seeing the words and understanding their far-reaching symptoms is usually something we just don't get. Let's take one brief look at the characteristic of depression. *DivorceCare* has effectively outlined the symptoms in a chapter of their workbook. Recognize any?[3]

Common Symptoms of Depression:

* Unconnectedness
* Profound sense of sadness
* Hopelessness, pessimism
* Guilt, worthlessness, helplessness
* No longer enjoy favorite activities
* Sleep patterns disturbed

* Change in eating habits
* Substantial loss of energy
* Entertain thoughts of suicide
* Restlessness and irritability
* Unable to concentrate
* Headaches
* Impact on spiritual life

(Note: The above list is not intended to relate to clinical depression which should be addressed by a mental health-care professional.)

> *"I remember sitting in my small group in DivorceCare as we analyzed the symptoms of depression. Wow. I had no idea of the range it encompassed! I always viewed depression as mainly being sad, down in the dumps, you know—depressed! I saw a lot of me on that list, and knowing what it was, depression; I could now take the steps needed to go through it the right way."*
>
> **Steven – Columbus, OH**

> *"I was so restless and irritable! That didn't feel like depression to me, but there it was on that list. We each talked about what we had experienced, and when it finally was my turn I told the group I had no idea that what I was experiencing had to do with depression! The only name I had given it was, 'I'm going through divorce.' Not to clear on what I was feeling, was I? Then the time came for us to talk about meaningful ways to deal with depression, and I took really great notes!"*
>
> **Eva – Grand Rapids, MI**

The way to avoid this *Pitfall* is to *not* stay unaware of what you are or will be going through. The fact that you can identify some of the details of your feelings and behavior will then allow you to effectively take steps to work through them. The books, tapes, and support groups previously mentioned will help you in your search to identify the common symptoms one experiences during separation. They will also provide practical techniques others have used to get them through these same areas.

I emphasize getting *through*, not *around*. We all want to get around them, avoid them, by-pass them, but it doesn't work. Once you realize that, then you can effectively go *through* them.

Working through specific separation symptoms involves the following:

1. *Knowing* the various unique separation symptoms.
2. *Identifying* which ones apply to you right *now*.
3. *Learning and applying* principles and techniques to successfully help you go through these unique symptoms. (*Start*)
4. Learning what *increases or feeds* these unique symptoms and taking steps to *avoid* doing those things. (*Stop*)

Jasmine was struck with how simple working through her separation symptoms could be at times.

"I started to laugh as he identified what we do to ourselves to increase the symptoms of anger. 'What's so funny?' he asked, as those in my small group turned toward me in anticipation of my answer. 'It's just so darn accurate! I've been doing exactly what I should

not *be doing, which in turn is making me angrier! I'm doing the very thing I don't want to happen to me—making me worse!'*

"*My classmates nodded their heads as if to not only understand but to signify that they, too, were guilty of the same mistake—feeding their anger—like putting logs into a fire.*

"*Our small-group facilitator had wisely told us to identify our thoughts and actions when we feel our symptoms of anger increasing.*

"*Well, I knew one action I was doing right off the bat! It was when I drove by my husband's girlfriend's house (yes, girlfriend!—the one ten years younger than him), only to see his car out front. That sends me over the edge! But now I know that. Really know it! If I simply put a stop to that activity, it would stop me from episodes of going 'over the edge.' Not that there aren't other issues I deal with, but this was definitely one I could begin to control. Stop driving by her house!*

"*It seemed so clear, so obvious, so basic as I sat there in the small group that night. 'Stop feeding my anger!'*"

Jasmine – Norfolk, VA

Knowing what feeds anger, depression, loneliness, unforgiveness, and the like is vital to helping us through these key areas. How about you? Can you identify the thoughts or actions that you sense increase or feed the symptoms of any of those four areas? How would you answer the following? Really try to stop for a moment and answer these.

THOUGHTS

When I **THINK** about the following (*Be specific*): **Fill in blank**.

(_____)

I **FEED** *or* **INCREASE** my: **Select best answer.**

* Anger * Depression * Loneliness * Unforgiveness

ACTIONS

When I **DO** the following (*Be specific*): **Fill in blank.**

(_____)

I **FEED** *or* **INCREASE** my: **Select best answer.**

* Anger * Depression * Loneliness * Unforgiveness

Identifying the specific things you *think* about and *do* that trigger increases in certain feelings will help you to better control those experiences. As **Jasmine** said, "*Stop driving by her house!*"

Brent also came away with a better understanding of his own situation after one of the seminar sessions at DivorceCare. Is it something you can relate to, not so much in the details, but in the lessons learned?

> "*I knew I was still bitter. So did most everyone else around me—my friends, co-workers, anyone with ears on their head! But knowing why it lingered was not as clear.*

Oh, the lies, the excuses for her being out late, the sense of betrayal were all part of my bitterness. That part was clear. Like her using the kids to visit his kids seemed so innocent. They were our neighbors just up the street. We had socials together, barbeques, kids' birthday parties together, me and my wife, him and his wife. I just had no idea my wife was seeing him in the guise of all this. My wife slept with a 'friend'! Sure I was bitter; it had been going on for months, she finally told me. Yeah that made me bitter and angry, but what was underneath all that? That night I soon discovered exactly the source of my bitterness.

"As I sat in our small group, the real issue became crystal clear: unforgiveness. I had never dealt with my not forgiving her. The truth of the matter is, I didn't want to forgive her! That would be letting her off the hook. That would be too easy. Too...well, forgiving!

"But I sat there as if scales on my eyes were lifted. I was bitter and angry because I had not forgiven her. Nor did I know how to—at least up to that moment. That was about to change, too.

"Hearing the answers of the others in the group on key questions our group leader was asking helped each of us to search deeper to better understand our own situation. My discovery led me to the need to forgive.

*"That night I came to find out what real forgiveness **is** and **is not**. I learned how unforgiveness affects me a thousand times more than it ever would her—to whom it was aimed at!*

"During that session, I wrote down and still review that list we were shown about forgiveness:

   * *Forgiveness doesn't mean you start trusting your partner as before.*

* *Forgiveness doesn't mean they deserve to be forgiven.*
* *Forgiveness isn't a feeling.*
* *Forgiveness is not pretending you're not hurt.*
* *Forgiveness is not saying what the other person did was not wrong.*
* *Forgiveness is not releasing the other person of responsibility.*

"*I sat there that night discovering that for me, my situation was the very personal issue of unforgiveness. I learned to my amazement what forgiveness **was not**. Then I learned what it **really is**. That's when my bitterness began to loosen its grip; my anger's fire was subdued. I was clearly seeing a change in me, for me, for my kids and all who knew me! This was the start of making a real day-to-day difference in my attitude, behavior, and general outlook.*

"*That was seven months ago. My wife filed for divorce, and my 'neighbor friend' has filed for divorce from his spouse. We live such messed-up lives. I've seen and heard of stuff like this for years. But not me, not my wife! How we all got here, that's another story, but going through this without intense bitterness or anger due to unforgiveness makes a major difference. I continue to forgive both her and him. It's not always easy, but you have no idea how I used to feel and react.*

"*I still have deep emotions about everything we're going through, but I know and those around me know the difference **within** me.*

Brent – Milwaukee, WI

Not being *aware* of separation's unique symptoms is a major *Pitfall*. This chapter points you in the right direction, but other resources, authors, and programs like *DivorceCare* will show you exactly what they are and both what to do and what not to do. Whatever it takes, just stay *aware* of *separation's unique symptoms*. Doing so will greatly help you during your time on this road of separation.

Scriptural Insights: Ch.4
Separation Symptoms? Not Aware of Any!

Ephesians 4:32 And be kind to one another, tenderhearted, forgiving each other, just as God also in Christ forgave you. **Matthew 6:12** Forgive us our debts, as we also forgive our debtors. **Matthew 6:14-15** "For if you forgive men their trespasses, your heavenly Father will also forgive you. **6:15** But if you don't forgive men their trespasses, neither will your Father forgive your trespasses. **Matthew 18:21-22** Then Peter came and said to him, "Lord, how often shall my brother sin against me, and I forgive him? Until seven times?" **18:22** Jesus said to him, "I don't tell you until seven times, but, until seventy times seven. **Psalm 37:8** Cease from anger, and forsake wrath. Don't fret, it leads only to evildoing. **Psalm 103:8** The LORD is merciful and gracious, slow to anger, and abundant in loving kindness. **Proverbs 16:32** One who is slow to anger is better than the mighty; one who rules his spirit, than he who takes a city. **Proverbs 19:11** The discretion of a man makes him slow to anger. It is his glory to overlook an offense. **Proverbs 22:8** He who sows wickedness reaps trouble, and the rod of his fury will be destroyed. **Ecclesiastes 7:9** Don't be hasty in your spirit to be angry, for anger rests in the bosom of fools. **Ephesians 4:26** "Be angry, and don't sin." Don't let the sun go down on your wrath **Psalm 34:4** I sought the LORD, and he answered me, and delivered me from all my fears. **Romans 12:19** Don't seek revenge yourselves, beloved, but give place to God's wrath. For it is written, "Vengeance belongs to me; I will repay, says the Lord." **James 1:19-20** So, then, my beloved brothers, let every man be swift to hear, slow to speak, and slow to anger; **1:20** for the anger of man doesn't produce the righteousness of God. **Philippians 4:13** I can do all things through Christ, who strengthens me. **Ephesians 4:31-32** Let all bitterness, wrath, anger, outcry, and slander, be put away from you, with all malice. **4:32** And be kind to one another, tenderhearted, forgiving each other, just as God also in Christ forgave you. **Hebrews 13:5-6** Be free from the love of money, content with such things as you have, for he has said, "I will in no way leave you, neither will I in any way forsake you." **13:6** So that with good courage we say, "The Lord is my helper. I will not fear. What can man do to me?" **Luke 6:27-28** "But I tell you who hear: love your enemies, do good to those who hate you, **6:28** bless those who curse you, and pray for those who mistreat you. **1 Peter 4:8** And above all things be earnest in your love among yourselves, for love covers a multitude of sins. **Isaiah 41:10** Don't you be afraid, for I am with you. Don't be dismayed, for I am your God. I will strengthen you. Yes, I will help you. Yes, I will uphold you with the right hand of my righteousness. **Proverbs 15:1** A gentle answer turns away wrath, but a harsh word stirs up anger. **Psalm 27:14** Wait for the LORD. Be strong, and let your heart take courage. Yes, wait for the LORD. **Psalm 42:11** Why are you in despair, my soul? Why are you disturbed within me? Hope in God! For I shall still praise him, the saving help of my countenance, and my God. **Psalm 55:22** Cast your burden on the LORD, and he will sustain you. He will never allow the righteous to be moved. **Matthew 28:20b** Behold, I am with you always, even to the end of the age." Amen.

Pitfall

5

◆ ◆ ◆

Not Deepening Your Spiritual Roots

Not deepening your spiritual roots to withstand the oncoming "storm" is never a healthy approach. It's one *Pitfall* you clearly want to avoid, but why it happens is understandable. Here are four typical reactions of people who are going through marital separation.

"God, you could have prevented this from happening!"

> * *Angry* with God, so one **stays away** from seeking God.

"God, you allowed this to happen, and I wish you hadn't!"

> * Still *feeling* God might have made the wrong choice, one is **hesitant** about seeking God.

"God, I know you give us free will. I know we do some stupid things. I know it grieves you that we made the choices we did to get us to this point."

> * *Knowing* a caring God can forgive, give strength and wisdom in *any* trial, one **seeks** Him for Divine intervention and help.

"God, I don't know if you're there and I've never really asked for your help in the past, but I need direction and strength to get through this one."

> * *Hoping* God is there, begins a **humble seeking** of Him for help.

If I were to ask you, *"Which of those four reactions toward God best describes you?"* what would you say? You might find that one squarely matches up to your situation, or it might be a little of this one and a little of that one. Either way, it's often hard *not* to think about God in some fashion during a major crisis in life, and *separation* just happens to be yours.

"When he said he wanted a divorce and left that night, I literally wept myself to sleep. But in between the tears, I cried out to God to please help me, help us, to not let this really happen."

Sarah – Tampa, FL

Vince describes his journey toward spiritual renewal:

"About two months had passed since she left me for another guy, and I still didn't know where we stood on divorce. Were we or not, going to go through with this? It was during that time that a guy from work invited me to attend his church on Sunday. It was his way of offering help and friendship, so I took him up on it. We had done a lot over the years, and I knew he was concerned. I'm so glad he took the effort to ask me! It helped me get back to God, church, and the Bible, something I hadn't done in a long time. I was starting to experience inner peace and strength in the midst of my messed-up, frustrated situation. Wow, what a difference it was making! I'm still going every Sunday and have even begun visiting a men's Bible study group during the week."

Vince – Detroit, MI

It's an amazing thing to consider the truth that a caring, loving God—*who has watched your entire life unfold from the time you were in your mother's womb until this very second*—really does care about you personally! This is about *relationship*, not religion.

Just as you have other relationships in your life, God wants to be one of them. We have heard story after story from those in separation who told us how they started a new or deeper relationship with God because of having experienced marital separation in their life.

As for them, so He extends His offer to *you* to come unto Him, to seek Him, to learn of Him, to know Him. Scripture states in the New Testament, *"Draw near to God and He will draw near to you."* (James 4:8) The bottom line is, God has never moved. He's always been there. It's you who has been moving in this direction, that direction. Now He's waiting and hoping you will take the next move in *His* direction in order for you to experience a deep relationship with Him. By doing so, you can gain a fresh start, a new heart, and the power to keep you strong for the upcoming, or ever present storm. What others have come to realize in a very real sense is: this really *is* about *relationship*, not religion. Knowing God *personally*, not just knowing *about* Him.

"I remember when the reality of our separation really started to sink in. How sick I felt about it. How ashamed and worthless I started to feel. I was seeing it beyond who was at fault. I was seeing the fact that here were two people who once loved each other so much that they wanted to and did everything to get married! Seeing that mountain top compared to this valley, made me shake my head in disbelief. But this was real. It was not going away. I needed help, but I was not sure where to turn.

"God had always been in my childhood upbringing but was pretty far from my adult life, let alone our marriage. I was going to change that by visiting a church in my neighborhood. That was the start of a renewal that has helped me in so many ways over the last four months. I just wish my wife had been seeking Him, too! But all I could do was work on me. I'm really glad I have been!"

Greg – Nashville, TN

For **Sarah**, **Vince**, and **Greg**, though their separations were for different reasons, they came to a point where they each realized that God was not just some church Sunday school story. He was and is God. He is living, all-knowing, and deeply concerned about each of us.

"I remember the night I prayed to God. I asked Him for forgiveness. I asked Him to take over my life. I told Him I believed His son Jesus died on the cross for all my sins. That I knew Jesus rose from the grave. I really believed all that, but now I needed to know God, really know Him, and to please come into my life and take it over. I needed help, and I wanted Him to be the main source of that help.

"That was eight months ago. The difference in my life, my views, my attitude, my understanding has completely changed. The separation became a divorce, but without Him I would be so miserably different. I really am seeing a new me! My kids can attest to that!"

Jennifer – Los Angeles, CA

A great website we found that can answer a lot of spiritual questions about who God is and how one can get closer to Him is found with a ministry organization called: *Back to the Bible*. Simply go to their Web address:

www.backtothebible.org

This is a wonderful ministry with lots of resources for those who want to go deeper in their faith. You'll find free Bible studies, real-life testimonies of fellow Christians, articles that will challenge you to grow, and a lot more! We hope you will visit and utilize its information on a regular basis. It all starts with *knowing* God, and they will show you how to do just that.

In a few key strokes you can begin taking action *against* **Pitfall #5 — *Not deepening your spiritual roots*.** We pray you do! This website is a great place to start:

www.backtothebible.org

Perhaps you see yourself as someone who has been a Christian for some time, knowing God *personally*, not just knowing *about* Him. But even as a Christian you feel distant from God. Maybe you wonder if your relationship will remain separated from Him like it is with your mate, due to things you have done. You might wonder if God will forgive you and help you establish a walk with Him again. **Bill** felt the same way.

"I knew it was wrong. I had told others in the same situation it was wrong. Wrong to yourself, your wife, your kids, your God, even for your reputation. But here I was, seeing another woman. It all happened so slowly, so seductively slow.

"When she joined my department in our company a year earlier, I was immediately drawn to her. Her appearance, her energy, her intellect, her wit and friendly, upbeat attitude were extremely pleasing to be around. We hit it off together from the start.

"Over the next twelve months, our time in committee meetings and work projects only deepened our mutual attraction toward each other. Her tossing out occasional sexual innuendoes to see my reactions brought us into a playful, but what I thought innocent, side of our growing friendship. It was only a matter of time that she began sharing intimate thoughts and feelings about her married life, of which she was increasingly dissatisfied with. Her successful husband seemed to have less and less time for her and the kids. And what little time they did have they never seemed to talk, talk about each other or their shared interest unless it was about the kids or the next planned family vacation. Hearing her be so open with me, I felt safe expressing my own doubts and troubles concerning my wife. Our frank discussions about our dried-out

marriages began to emotionally bond us. We both felt it happening, and others at work were taking notice of our growing closeness and occasional glances of playful romance on the rise.

"It was only a matter of time. We both knew we were dangerously approaching a place of no return. Six months later we found ourselves there, hopelessly infatuated and thinking of nothing else but about our next rendezvous—our next getaway.

"I laid there feeling relaxed but troubled. Guilt was taking hold of my conscience and soul. How could I, how could we, as two professing Christians, find ourselves doing what we knew was wrong? Doing what we knew was against everything we had heard in church, read in the Bible, and had ourselves taught in Sunday school from time to time? Despite this guilt, we both kept going to our separate churches each weekend, me with my wife and kids, her with her family at their church. Our family had been attending the neighborhood church for over ten years. She and her husband were more infrequent attendees to their church, but we both kept on going as if nothing was different.

"My guilt at first was strong, deep and searing. But her seductive ways and our need for sexual excitement and fulfillment kept bringing us back together. We convinced ourselves that it was always more than just sex between us. It was about being successful at work together, our conversations over coffee, her personality, and a hundred other things that were so luring, so desirable, things we both were missing at this level with our present mates. Still, the guilt came. But when I didn't see any lightening strikes from Heaven, and our spouses hadn't caught us, the guilt became less and less over time.

*"But time was about to run out. The day she told me was as if time stood still. Everything was in slow motion as she stumbled at first with her wording, looking down at the table where we were sitting. She then became more composed, and, looking steadily into my eyes, she told me she was leaving. Her husband got a transfer out on the West coast. A larger salary, more flexible time to be with her and the kids, and a 'new start for their marriage,' her husband told her. She paused, looking, what seemed like an eternity, in my eyes and said, 'I'm **not** going to leave him.' I just sat there in silence, gazing back at her. Dazed in unbelief, I just sat there looking at her. Then her eyes turned aside in our moment of truth.*

"At the peak of our affair, she was choosing him over me. Not that we had ever talked about it; there was never a need to. Even now, talking was not what this discussion was about. It was one of informing. Informing me that she had made up her mind, she was not willing to lose what she had with her husband, even if it wasn't the best marriage possible. She would move with her husband as a united family.

"When her words began to really sink in, she dropped another bomb on me. She felt that since this was definite, it would probably be best on both of us if we simply stopped seeing each other outside of work. I couldn't believe how controlled and matter-of-fact she was, as resolve took its focused hold on her demeanor. Much like I had seen her perform during past business negotiations with clients, business-like, confident, determined to get her way. We both knew she was right. It would be best to make a clean break, no matter how hard or painful. So we did.

"Those first few weeks after the breakup were indescribably painful. Then when she left the

company, and then our city, I really hit bottom. I felt truly alone. Three major events had decisively changed my life. My affair was halted, my wife months earlier had left me, having eventually found out about the affair, and then my work performance was at such a low point it was 'suggested' that I take a 'vacation' for a few weeks until I got my 'rest' and perspective back to where it needed to be. It was during those vacation weeks I started asking myself some tough questions. Questions about me, about what was really important to me. Where was I going? What did I really want to accomplish in my life? Questions I had lost touch with during my all-consuming affair. One thing I knew for sure was, my life was entering a new phase; it was changing, and I had no idea what it might entail.

"That time off from work positioned me for long-needed self-reflection. I got serious about my present and future. I knew I needed to make a fresh commitment to my wife and family. My wife had left town to stay with her parents in Upper State New York when everything broke open. She was in a supportive surrounding up there with our four-year-old twins. As a stay-at-home mom, she had the luxury of picking up and leaving as she did. I knew I needed to make things right with her and friends I had let down. I also knew if I was serious about a true life change, it would have to involve God, too. My family seemed much easier to fix than my walk with God. They only knew bits and pieces about the affair. God knew everything, every single detail of my thoughts, intents, and actions. Just thinking about all He knew, I felt a guilt I had long lost, I was overwhelmed with my sense of moral failure and sin. I had truly failed Him, and I could hardly lift my head up in His direction, feeling such deserved holy condemnation. My head bowed and my open weeping before Him 'to please help me get back on track' was the beginning of my healing.

"My desire to make things right with God was a journey in and of itself. Friends, my minister, books, and a men's Christian Conference at our church all played a role. The message of God's forgiveness, love, and concern for me kept coming through.

"'Bill,' my friend said as we sat across from each other in the corner of our favorite coffee shop, 'God knows that we make bad choices. He doesn't want us to; He knows the outcomes that happen when we do. But still, He's there, as a Father with open arms, welcoming us back. He's there. Understanding, sorry you failed, but forgiving, and strengthening, to give you a new start, a renewed hope that from here on out it will be different with His help!'

"Bill's words were comforting to me, but I still doubted if God would take me back and really forgive me. Not after what I had done. I had left Him and His commandments so deliberately, so blatantly. But over time I came to truly believe that He wanted to and did forgive me. I had left Him, but He was always there waiting for me. I sincerely came back, repentant, and He was there to forgive, renew, and help me back on my feet. He has done that in so many ways. In each area of my life I began to see progress as I did my part on making things right. I especially focused on my wife.

"We're still separated. She's in a wait-and-see mode, to see if this change of heart is real. I know it is, thanks to God. In time, she will, too."

Bill – Manhattan, NY

Is **Bill's** story something you can relate to? Maybe not in the exact details, but do you as a Christian, in this time of marital separation, find yourself feeling God won't forgive you for some bad decisions on your part? As with **Bill**, God *does* forgive as only God can forgive.

Kathy and I made some bad choices during our previous marriages and during our times of marital separation from our previous mates. We know firsthand how God really can help restore you and lift the burden of guilt and set you on a renewed relationship with Him so that in *His* strength you will walk a new path. It first begins by you coming to Him with a broken and humble heart. Right where you are, you can express your deepest feelings of regret, confessing sins, asking for His forgiveness and help. His Word to us is so promising:

"If we confess our sins, He is faithful and just to forgive us our sins and to cleanse us from all unrighteousness."
(I John 1:9)

Even now, you could stop reading and pray to God about this. Then, at the right time, come back to read the rest of this chapter. He's right there, caring, hoping you will do just that. Stop, reflect, confess, and receive His forgiveness. *We'll wait for you.*

TIPS TO CONSIDER

Welcome back. We would further suggest you go deeper in your faith, especially to prepare you for the present and upcoming storms found on this road of separation.

The following tips have been voiced by many who *have* gone deeper. Could one or more of these be something you could begin working on? Having a game plan of what to do is the first step. These tips could give you that sense of direction; the rest is up to you. Deepening your spiritual roots is a slow yet steady process. Here's how to begin:

Tip #1: Seek advice from godly and wise Christians. The world's perspective and God's are usually at opposite ends of the spectrum. It's easy to find the world's advice from those around us such as our sincere non-Christian friends, relatives, or co-workers, but the effort to be picky about receiving and acting on godly advice is worth the effort. (If the Christian is also experienced in separation and divorce, the advice will be especially helpful!) An additional source for godly advice is from your local pastor or Christian counselor.

Tip #2: Keep asking yourself, "What does the Bible say about this or that issue, about my choice of action or thought?" As you approach each day, you need to ask and find out what Scripture has to say about your everyday problems, pain, actions, and thoughts. As practicing Christians, we can know the will of God in all matters, because He left a guidebook, a set of instructions, when He provided us the Holy Bible. It's extremely practical and not just a history lesson that some have seen it to be. God speaks to us on "*separation*" issues such as guilt, forgiveness, revenge, depression, finances, fear, love, and hate, from the use of our words to the thoughts we should focus on in our heads.

Tip #3: Commit to attending a Bible-believing church at least once a week. This is an important part of deepening your spiritual roots. You will experience a time of worship and praise, a time of fellowship with other believers, and a time of hearing God's Word. If you feel embarrassed, judged, or uncomfortable attending your *own* church, simply decide to go elsewhere for a period of time. The important thing will be that you are going and not withdrawing from the Church that God has established. His House is for His believers to worship Him and learn of Him from His Word, a place of refuge and spiritual strengthening for His children, like you, having accepted Jesus as your personal Savior. If after a period of time you feel comfortable going back to your own church, then you will. But going to a Bible-believing church *somewhere* each week is what's important. Some have even found going more than once a week to be of great help, especially during this phase of separation.

Tip #4: Find a few minutes each day for personal Bible reading and prayer. These daily devotions can be like cool water in a parched desert. It doesn't need to take long. Maybe you've never done this before or you've gotten out of the habit. Either way, many have found a five-minute devotional time of Bible reading and prayer at the start of each day to be a real strength for what lies ahead.

Bible Reading: Many have found reading from the Psalms to be most helpful. Read one entire Old Testament Psalm, or read for two to three minutes. Then, the other two to three minutes can be for your prayer time. The website **www.backtothebible.org** also provides many guides for these types of morning devotions. Listening to the Bible on audio cassette/CD when driving to work or wherever is also recommended (available at most secular and Christian bookstores or websites).

Prayer: During your prayer time, begin by thanking God for what you do have, for who *He is*. Next, pray specifically for others, then your own situation. These steps will prove to be a good pattern for morning devotions. Also, praying simple prayers of thanks and requests *throughout the day* is definitely a way to be walking in the Spirit, for He's always there! *It's about relationship, not religion. Talk* to Him, share your heart. He cares. It's called *prayer*. Doing it has proved extremely helpful to those who have gone before you on this road of separation.

Tip #5: Meditate on one new Scripture verse every week. If possible, even memorize it. As you spend time each day reading the Scriptures, you will occasionally come across a verse that's especially meaningful. Simply write it down on a 3x5 card and keep it with you in the car, at home in the kitchen, wherever you will be able to glance at it. Some even put it next to the mirror in the bathroom to look at while shaving or putting on make-up. The goal, of course, is to see it, read it, review it, think about it. For some of you, it might be a verse worth memorizing. If you do choose to memorize, we suggest you look for verses that are not only meaningful but are short, as well. One verse that was of special comfort to me during my separation was,

> *"Draw near to God and He will draw near to you."*
> (James 4:8)

A verse Kathy especially held onto during her separation was from the Old Testament book of Jeremiah:

> *"I know the plans I have for you, says the Lord, plans of hope and of a future."*
> (Jeremiah 29:11)

Another source for choosing Scripture verses to meditate on can be from Biblical Resource books found in Christian bookstores. Even in the back of many Bibles you will find a Topical Index that lists specific Scriptures according to topic (i.e. anger – then all the scripture verses that discuss anger are listed). Many Bible promises can be found, mediated on, and memorized to help deepen your spiritual roots.

So, do any of those tips have a chance in your life right now? Which ones? Starting today? If already applying them, could you increase just a little bit more? We hope so!

Not deepening your spiritual roots is one *Pitfall* you surely don't want to fall into. Let this time of trial be a time of renewal, also—a *spiritual* renewal. Many before you discovered such renewal for themselves when they were walking the road you're now on.

Looking ahead, our next ***Pitfall, #6,*** is about kids. **Please, please be sure to read this section—including those of you *without* kids.** This chapter will help deepen and broaden your view of this issue. It is well worth reading! God will use it in your life somehow, somewhere, maybe as you relate to a friend who does have kids or in relating to children whose parents are separated. But somehow, somewhere, God will use the contents of this next chapter in your life. Whether you do or don't have kids, don't miss the impact of these next few pages. Thanks for staying the course! You'll be glad you did.

Scriptural Insights: Ch.5
Not Deepening Your Spiritual Roots

2 Thessalonians 1:3 We are bound to always give thanks to God for you, brothers, even as it is appropriate, because your faith grows exceedingly, and the love of each and every one of you towards one another abounds; **1 Peter 2:2** as newborn babies, long for the pure milk of the Word, that you may grow thereby **2 Peter 3:18** But grow in the grace and knowledge of our Lord and Savior Jesus Christ. To him be the glory both now and forever. Amen. **Deuteronomy 4:29** But from there you shall seek the LORD your God, and you shall find him, when you search after him with all your heart and with all your soul. **1 Chronicles 22:19a** Now set your heart and your soul to seek after the LORD your God. **Psalm 14:2** The LORD looked down from heaven on the children of men, to see if there were any who did understand, who did seek after God. **Psalm 63:1** God, you are my God. I will earnestly seek you. My soul thirsts for you. My flesh longs for you, in a dry and weary land, where there is no water. **Matthew 6:33** But seek first God's Kingdom, and his righteousness; and all these things will be given to you as well. **Colossians 3:1-2** If then you were raised together with Christ, seek the things that are above, where Christ is, seated on the right hand of God. **3:2** Set your mind on the things that are above, not on the things that are on the earth. **Hebrew 11:6** Without faith it is impossible to be well pleasing to him, for he who comes to God must believe that he exists, and that he is a rewarder of those who seek him. **Galatians 3:26** For you are all children of God, through faith in Christ Jesus. **Ephesians 5:1** Be therefore imitators of God, as beloved children. **Isaiah 42:16** I will bring the blind by a way that they don't know. I will lead them in paths that they don't know. I will make darkness light before them, and crooked places straight. I will do these things, and I will not forsake them. **Hebrews 13:7** Remember your leaders, men who spoke to you the word of God, and considering the results of their conduct, imitate their faith. **Hebrews 10:25** not forsaking our own assembling together, as the custom of some is, but exhorting one another; and so much the more, as you see the Day approaching. **Psalm 119:114** You are my hiding place and my shield. I hope in your word. **Psalm 119:105** Your word is a lamp to my feet, and a light for my path. **Psalm 119:11** I have hidden your word in my heart, that I might not sin against you. **Psalm 31:14-15** But I trust in you, LORD. I said, "You are my God." **31:15** My times are in your hand. Deliver me from the hand of my enemies, and from those who persecute me. **Psalm 1:1-3** Blessed is the man who doesn't walk in the counsel of the wicked, nor stand in the way of sinners, nor sit in the seat of scoffers; **1:2** but his delight is in the LORD'S law. On his law he meditates day and night. **1:3** He will be like a tree planted by the streams of water, that brings forth its fruit in its season, whose leaf also does not wither. Whatever he does shall prosper. **Proverbs 28:13-14** He who conceals his sins doesn't prosper, but whoever confesses and renounces them finds mercy. **28:14** Blessed is the man who always fears; but one who hardens his heart falls into trouble. **Psalm 37:7** Rest in the LORD, and wait patiently for him. Don't fret because of him who prospers in his way, because of the man who makes wicked plots happen. **Psalm 37:23-24** A man's goings are established by the LORD. He delights in his way. **37:24** Though he stumble, he shall not fall, for the LORD holds him up with his hand. **Isaiah 41:10** Don't you be afraid, for I am with you. Don't be dismayed, for I am your God. I will strengthen you. Yes, I will help you. Yes, I will uphold you with the right hand of my righteousness. **Isaiah 55:6-7** Seek the LORD while he may be found; call you on him while he is near **55:7** let the wicked forsake his way, and the unrighteous man his thoughts; and let him return to the LORD, and he will have mercy on him; and to our God, for he will abundantly pardon. **Isaiah 40:28-31** Haven't you known? Haven't you heard? The everlasting God, the LORD, The Creator of the ends of the earth, doesn't faint. He isn't weary. His understanding is unsearchable. **40:29** He gives power to the weak. He increases the strength of him who has no might. **40:30** Even the youths faint and get weary, and the young men utterly fall; **40:31** But those who wait for the LORD will renew their strength. They will mount up with wings like eagles. They will run, and not be weary. They will walk, and not faint. **Romans 15:4-5** For whatever things were written before were written for our learning, that through patience and through encouragement of the Scriptures we might have hope. **15:5** Now the God of patience and of encouragement grant you to be of the same mind one with another according to Christ Jesus. **Romans 5:8-10** But God commends his own love toward us, in that while we were yet sinners, Christ died for us. **Romans 5:9** Much more then, being now justified by his blood, we will be saved from God's wrath through him. **5:10** For if, while we were enemies, we were reconciled to God through the death of his Son, much more, being reconciled, we will be saved by his life. **Romans 12:1-2** Therefore I urge you, brothers, by the mercies of God, to present your bodies a living sacrifice, holy, acceptable to God, which is your spiritual service. **12:2** Don't be conformed to this world, but be transformed by the renewing of your mind, so that you may prove what is the good, well-pleasing, and perfect will of God. **Hebrews 13:5-6** Be free from the love of money, content with such things as you have, for he has said, "I will in no way leave you, neither will I in any way forsake you." **13:6** So that with good courage we say, "The Lord is my helper. I will not fear. What can man do to me?" **John 5:24** "Most certainly I tell you, he who hears my word, and believes him who sent me, has eternal life, and doesn't come into judgment, but has passed out of death into life. **2 Chronicles 7:14** If my people, who are called by my name, shall humble themselves, and pray, and seek my face, and turn from their wicked ways; then will I hear from heaven, and will forgive their sin, and will heal their land. **Jeremiah 17:7** Blessed is the man who trusts in the LORD, and whose trust the LORD is. **Jeremiah 29:11-13** For I know the thoughts that I think toward you, says the LORD, thoughts of peace, and not of evil, to give you hope and a future. **29:12** You shall call on me, and you shall go and pray to me, and I will listen to you. **29:13** You shall seek me, and find me, when you shall search for me with all your heart. **1 John 1:5-10** This is the message which we have heard from him and announce to you, that God is light, and in him is no darkness at all. **1:6** If we say that we have fellowship with him and walk in the darkness, we lie, and don't tell the truth. **1:7** But if we walk in the light, as he is in the light, we have fellowship with one another, and the blood of Jesus Christ, his Son, cleanses us from all sin. **1:8** If we say that we have no sin, we deceive ourselves, and the truth is not in us. **1:9** If we confess our sins, he is faithful and righteous to forgive us the sins, and to cleanse us from all unrighteousness. **1:10** If we say that we haven't sinned, we make him a liar, and his word is not in us. **James 4:8a** Draw near to God, and he will draw near to you. **Proverbs 3:5-6** Trust in the LORD with all your heart, and don't lean on your own understanding. **3:6** In all your ways acknowledge him, and he will make your paths straight. **Colossians 1:9** For this cause, we also, since the day we heard this, don't cease praying and making requests for you, that you may be filled with the knowledge of his will in all spiritual wisdom and understanding **James 1:5** But if any of you lacks wisdom, let him ask of God, who gives to all liberally and without reproach; and it will be given to him. **Philippians 4:6-7** In nothing be anxious, but in everything, by prayer and petition with thanksgiving, let your requests be made known to God. **4:7** And the peace of God, which surpasses all understanding, will guard your hearts and your thoughts in Christ Jesus. **1 Peter 5:5-7** "God resists the proud, but gives grace to the humble." **5:6** Humble yourselves therefore under the mighty hand of God, that he may exalt you in due time; **5:7** casting all your worries on him, because he cares for you.

SocietyD.com
When You
Separate or Divorce

6 Pitfall

◆ ◆ ◆

My Kids Are Fine—
Kids Bounce Back!

The research is out, and it's not promising. Separation and divorce impact our kids—period.[1] We all know it to be true but hope for the best: "They'll bounce back—kids are like that!" or so we tell ourselves, and that's the *Pitfall*, believing that "*kids just bounce back.*"

Our children primarily become affected *emotionally*, and their age *does* vary the effect (preschool, ages five to eight, ages nine to twelve, teenagers, and grown children). Differences between how boys react versus girls can also be distinct. The symptoms of that effect can be immediate, short term, and long term—with varying degrees based on lots of variables, which can best be found from other resources (books, CDs, articles, etc.).

Knowing that separation does affect them, *visible or not*, should cause us to be on the alert and to take action to help them through this phase—whether or not divorce ever happens.

If separation is the third major stress circumstance listed for *adults*[2], can you honestly think it's *not* going to impact your children? Of course you don't. It's really a question of what you should *begin doing* or *stop doing* to reduce your children's stress levels.

Emotional responses from children can range from anger, loss of self-esteem, depression, withdrawal, aggressiveness, to denial.

> *"When my six-year-old began to withdraw from activities I knew he enjoyed, it worried me, so I did some reading. A magazine article described various symptoms which can occur during family crises, and this clearly was a crisis. He hadn't seen his dad in weeks and would only begin doing so every few days. Not seeing his dad spend the night anymore really took its toll. Is his father a deceiving cheat, an unfaithful husband? Yes, but he was a good father and especially a great storyteller at night with his son."*
> **Sandra – Jacksonville, FL**

> *"My daughters were more moody now than before all this happened. They were having their normal sister rivalry, but it was clearly up quite a few notches. Things set them off much too easily, directed both*

*toward me and each other. I would make simple
requests for them to do something, and I always got an
argument about it. You can't tell me that they aren't
feeling their lives coming unglued as they see their
parents tear apart the family unit!"*

Larry – Minneapolis, MN

MISTAKES PARENTS MAKE

The role parents take in their children's lives
during this separation phase can help either ease the
crisis or make it worse for their kids. Mistakes
parents can make during this time that do *not* help
are listed in a *DivorceCare* publication.[3] They
include (with added clarifications):

* **Criticizing the other parent** (to the children
  directly or within hearing distance of the kids—
  via phone conversations or adults talking in the
  other room)
* **Using children as spies** (to report what the other
  parent is doing when returning from a visit)
* **Using the children as messengers** ("Tell your
  father, he'd better...")
* **Restricting visitation** (making it tough for the
  other parent to see them: "The kids' child
  support is late, so no kids!" "They have
  homework, chores, just sat down to eat a meal,
  been bad so they can't go out, whatever!")
* **Making too many changes that impact the
  children**
* **Forcing kids to choose** (on issues that make
  them choose for or against Dad or Mom—
  holidays, special days, legal issues, whatever

appears to benefit one parent and makes the other the loser)

* **Making promises you can't keep** (these especially happen with visiting fathers)
* **One of the parents enters a premature new relationship with the opposite sex**
* **Custody battles or other court-related issues mentioned in front of the kids**
* **Allowing a loss of structure** (schedules, normal day-to-day patterns of lifestyle)
* **Spiritual beliefs ignored or simply not practiced** (kids see this in parents)

Can you relate to anything on that list? It might be a mistake worth correcting. Go ahead, really look over this list and ask yourself what you've witnessed or been a part of over this time of your separation. Ask yourself, "Have I…," then reflect on your answer.

Have I criticized the other parent in the hearing of my children?
Yes / No
Have I used the children as spies at any time?
Yes / No
Have I used the children as messengers?
Yes / No
Have I restricted visitation or time in any way?
Yes / No
Have I made too many changes that are impacting the kids?
Yes / No
Have I put the children in positions that forced them to choose?
Yes / No

Have I made promises to the kids I can't keep?
Yes / No
Have I entered a premature new relationship with the opposite sex?
Yes / No
Have I mentioned court-related issues in front of or to the kids?
Yes / No
Have I allowed a loss of structure with the children?
Yes / No
Have I ignored or simply not practiced many of my spiritual beliefs?
Yes / No

Doing the above exercise is a sobering way to confront yourself with how you are dealing with your children right now or how you did in the recent past. Mistakes you *can* avoid. If you find yourself "guilty" of these mistakes, you can choose *not* to repeat them. You can ask for forgiveness from those faulted and from God. You *can* do this better, in varying degrees, at various times, but moving toward improvement, not harm.

Kathy and I look back and see how, in our times of separation from our previous mates, we too, were "guilty" of some of those *listed* mistakes. Many times we were simply unaware of what we were doing; other times we knew exactly the mistakes we were making but did them anyway, out of anger or revenge or for a million other reasons. But when we each reached the point of understanding *clearly* what mistakes we were making, and the harm it was causing, we began the process of change. We consciously chose to improve those areas with God's help—the very thing *you* can do if you decide to. Nobody said it's easy, but only that it's important. It's right. It's vital for our children's development.

> *"I simply didn't have the energy to fight this battle with my husband **and** maintain the kids like I was used to. I was letting so much slide that before all this separation took place I would never, I mean never, have allowed the kids to get away with. Not cleaning their rooms, slack on most chores, their eating habits, watching too much TV. Most of the 'norms' were falling apart, and it was showing!"*
>
> **Rachel – Albuquerque, NM**

> *"Did I ever in a million years think she would be out till all hours of the night with her 'friends'? Hardly! But it was really upsetting me. Yes, I love my kids. Yes, I don't mind watching them—they are my kids! But nearly every Friday and Saturday night was getting to be too much, and I wasn't shy expressing my feelings to the kids, either. They were teens, and they could take the truth. If they had a different view of their mom because of her weekend of partying, that wasn't my fault. It was her life she was living, and I was simply acknowledging it!"*
>
> **Scott – Houston, TX**

Helping our kids *through* this separation phase or *adding to their stress* of it is up to us. In little and big ways, day in and day out, we *can* make a difference for our kids.

Maybe this separation will lead to divorce and then everything becomes even *more* impacting, but we have to remember they are the innocent party here. They feel powerless in changing what they see happening before their very eyes. In our adult eyes, thinking about our pain, our disillusionment over our failed marriage, it's easy to focus on YOU, mainly YOU, completely on YOU. Meanwhile, our kids get only our upset, over-reactive attitudes or a response that is withdrawn and depressed—rarely one that is balanced.

Yes, you love them, but they know you are consumed with the details of this separation, and they are feeling the side effects—the separation shock waves. They need more than a roof over their heads and three square meals a day. They need us to *do* and *not do* certain things during this incredibly challenging time in their life. *Their life.*

> *"I saw myself withdraw from so much. I stopped going to church—embarrassed about my failed marriage that no one ever suspected. I stopped going out with friends—they were all married. I watched a lot of TV and spent a lot time in my bedroom—crying! How could I begin to think about my kids? It was like I had zoned out completely. If the kids weren't fighting, I figured all was well. I lived that way for months! I feel guilty now that I think about it. I'm just glad I somehow got refocused on them."*
>
> **Patricia – Mobile, AL**

> *"When my brother went through his divorce, I couldn't believe how little time he spent with his three kids! He loved those kids. Talking to him about it years later, he told me how much pain he experienced when after only a few hours of playing ball with them he'd drop them off at their mom's house and on the way back to his own place he'd cry like crazy. The pain of loss was so great. That pain happened every time he was with them. He'd delay seeing them*

sometimes by consuming his time at work or time out with friends just not to experience that pain. Sounds crazy, but that's what he said.

"Then, my time came. I was the one in marital separation, and I was the one visiting my kids. I now knew what my brother was experiencing and talking about, but I was determined not to do the same. I stepped over that pain and chose to do whatever I could to see my kids all the time, any time but to see them, call them, or email them. I might be separated from my wife, but I will not be separated from my kids when I have a say in it!"

Thomas – Cleveland, OH

There's a lot of great advice available to you if you simply take the effort to research it; advice about every possible issue as it *relates to children* when their parents are going through a separation or divorce. It is advice filled with professional and personal perspectives.

Even those who have gone through separation *as* children of divorced parents and now are full-grown adults themselves can each give practical insight to guide you in what you'll want to look out for, things to be sure *to do* and what you want to *keep from doing*. Our kids need us to listen to this advice and step up to the plate for them. If they knew what was really happening to them, they would especially ask us to do this for them.

"As an adult who now remembers what it was like to see my parents go through a separation then a divorce, I have plenty of advice. One thing that stands out to me is: Don't share every detail with us (as kids). Things like legal details. Mom got so angry and upset after opening the mail to discover another court

hearing was ordered, and then she would go off on how mean and awful a person Dad was to be doing this to her. It was so one-sided! I tried not to take sides, but Mom's emotional state made me want to hug her and hate Dad. I didn't even know, till much later, that he was simply fighting for more time to spend with us kids!"

Juan – Miami, FL

Janet has her own views, too, as she looks back to when she was a child of separation.

"Now in my late thirties, I look back and remember painfully how bad a divorce my parents had. If they had kept even half of it out of our sight, I think it would have made a huge difference. I felt so unsure about their love as I saw them so consumed with what was going on with them.

"I was an afterthought. At least that's how I felt. As a kid it's never about truth, it's about perception, it's about feelings.

"During my parents' marital separation, my time with Dad was less and less. They were simple moments at some fast-food restaurant or a walk through the mall, where he always bought me something—something he never did when we were a complete family (unless it was a special occasion). So our time together went by much too fast, only to be dropped off back at home with Mom. Their hate for each other scared me. Could they hate me, too? Love had turned to hate with them, why not me next? That's what I was thinking at age seven. A child's mind is such a fragile thing!"

Janet – Harvard, CN

The message we've often heard from now grown children of divorce is, *"Parents, do divorce right—*

correctly in front of the kids. Be mindful of what they see and hear. It's not about them—it's about the parents, so keep it to the parents" (the facts and the emotions).

As my wife, Kathy, and I have worked with leaders and individuals in Separation and Divorce Recovery over the years, we've picked up some great *"Quick Tips"* to keep parents on target. These insights might be helpful, in a practical sense, for those of you with kids.

QUICK TIPS

Quick Tip #1: See the world through your child's eyes. When your kids are not around, simply go into one of their bedrooms. Sit on the bed. Then, in the quietness of the moment, look around the room. Really absorb their world for a moment. Imagine you are them by "becoming" your child sitting on the bed. That is your room. Imagine your parents (you and your spouse) exchanging words in the hallway. Imagine you overhearing their plans on the pending divorce. Imagine the uncertainty of your future, how your life will be forever changed. No more *us*. No more *family* as you've always known it. Imagine being afraid, of dealing with all of this, your feelings, your life, your future—how it's all so unsure.

This tip will help you see better from your child's eyes, perspective, and feelings.

Quick Tip #2: When your mate telephones and your kids are nearby, *never* over react to your mate's comments. Instead, react knowing you have an audience—your kids. If it's something simple, no problem; they can hear your response to what time your spouse needs to be by to pick them up. But if it's heated or emotional in content, take it to another room, in private. Minimize what your children hear and see you do when that phone rings. This is between *parents*, not kids.

This tip really helps reduce stress in the children. The kids love both of you. Strengthen that by not letting them feel bad toward one over the other by what they hear and see you do when the phone rings.

Quick Tip #3: This one is for the visiting parent— usually the Dad. Don't buy and spend every time you pick up your kids. They want *you*, time with you, not purchases.

What you are doing gets really obvious as the days, weeks, months, and years pass by. Find creative *free* things to do. Spend time with them at the parks, throwing ball or Frisbees; washing the car together, playing cards or board games; popping corn and watching a rental video. It's not going to the *expensive* outings of movies, video game parks, super slides, eating out, and Disney World, of buying something new each and every time they are with you. Spending money does *not* prove that you really, really love them. *Time* with them does. Even doing mundane chores together, going grocery shopping, picking up dry cleaning—the same things they do with the other parent! Time with you is not always "happy" time as much as *everyday living*. And yes, sometimes that *is* sprinkled with "happy" times! Just be real. Live real life.

Also, don't promise what you'll do the next time you're together. If you're going to do it, surprise them by doing it; don't disappoint them by *not* doing it, no matter how small or great the *next time* events will be. Just tell them how you look forward to *being with* them next time.

This tip will help to keep your time with your kids more *normal*, which is needed now. It also does *not* create opportunities for more major disappointments. *No promises!*

(We would add that the above Tip #3 is also for the Custodial Parent in that they should be careful not to compete with the Visiting Parent if that parent is showering the kids with gifts. Don't try to match their actions. Instead, as mentioned above, spending time with your kids is key. Attend as many sporting events, school meetings dealing with them, watch them lift weights or practice the piano, have their friends over for tacos and make cookies together. This will bond you to your kids and allow them to talk to you about what is on their minds.)

Quick Tip #4: During your everyday activities (apart from telephone calls), you need to experience your deep emotions about your separation in *private*. Yes, you're hurting or angry or depressed. That is *your* world. Don't add those feelings to what your kids are already experiencing on their own. Every time you allow them to see and feel *your* pain, you are adding to a child's burden, which is already more than they need. Will they see and hear your emotions? Yes, but *minimize* it, please, for their emotional well being and in order not to divide their loyalty. They will feel sorry for you and want to protect you from more of that pain and therefore will reflect that toward the other parent. Some children actually build unwarranted hate toward another parent based solely on the emotional response of the hurting parent. Our children should not be put through this, and the way to help prevent it is by minimizing what they see *you* feel.

This tip will shield your children from added emotional burdens and build loyalty to both parents as they go through this separation.

Quick Tip #5: Help and encourage the children to honor the other parent on special days such as birthdays, Mother's Day, Father's Day, and other holidays. Remind the children, encourage them, and help them to make, buy, or do whatever they need to do to express their love at those times. They're kids and will forget, no matter how much they love the parent. So they need parental reminders. This should be on the mind of each parent as such special days approach.

Also, encourage your kids to do "random acts of kindness" for the other parent. Dad, you might tell your kids to do this for their mother: *"Just go up to Mom, hug her, and tell her how much you love her—she'll love that!"* Or Mom, you might encourage your kids like this: *"Why don't you email your Father and tell him how good you did on that test at school—he'd love to hear about it!"* Even if you and the other parent are in a real hateful, bitter, they-don't-deserve-kindness type of relationship, still encourage your *children* to love them, to really be loving by performing random acts of kindness for the other parent.

This tip helps strengthen the child-parent relationship but also shows the child that both parents still care about the other. They are not enemies, even if the parents think so!

Quick Tip #6: Speak positively, *not* negatively about the other parent to or around your kids. When your friends drop by or call on the phone, or when your relatives or co-workers drop by or call, don't talk in negative terms about the other parent within hearing distance of the kids. Get creative and change the subject. This not only applies with others but also when talking out loud to *yourself.* If something happens and it "sets you off," don't start talking to yourself out loud so the kids hear it. When you do talk negatively, you see it as talking about your spouse, but the kids hear it as talking about their father or mother.

If, in the past, your kids were at a friend's house and heard someone talking negatively about their parents, they would be hurt. That's from *outside* the home. How much more hurtful is it for them to hear it from the other parent! Don't divide the loyalty or harm the child's impression of the other parent. Protect. Build up. *The problem is between the parents, not between the parent and child.* Keep it that way. The parents will always be the parents, even twenty-five years later, and impressions are hard to erase. Keep the battle of negative words *only* between the parents. Don't scar the kids, no matter how "truthful" you think you're being about the other parent. They'll form their own opinions as they grow older. They see much more than you think! But they don't need your help getting there. *Shield, don't share.*

This tip protects the parent-child relationship for now *and* the years ahead.

These six quick tips are proven, practical suggestions learned by the failure and successes of those ahead of you on this road of separation. They hope you will consider them, too.

Separation is always painful, but there are degrees of doing things, which can lead to lesser or greater pain, which in turn can lead to more negative or positive effects, both now, soon after, or later on in our children's lives.

Positive effects won't just happen because "they're kids and kids bounce back, kids are resilient." They will happen because you as a loving parent went beyond your own pain and disillusionment to focus on the little and big things that will make a difference for them. For their sake, *don't* believe this deceiving ***Pitfall #6: My kids are fine. Kids bounce back.***

Years from now, you'll especially know why. Years from now, so will your children.

Some exceptionally good websites to assist you in raising your children include: **www.family.org** and **www.familylife.com**.

Scriptural Insights: Ch.6
My Kids are Fine—Kids Bounce Back!

Proverbs 6:20 My son, keep your father's commandment, and don't forsake your mother's teaching. **Ephesians 6:1** Children, obey your parents in the Lord, for this is right. **Ephesians 3:20** Children, obey your parents in all things, for this pleases the Lord. **Deuteronomy 6:1-2** Now this is the commandment, the statutes, and the ordinances, which the LORD your God commanded to teach you, that you might do them in the land where you go over to possess it; **6:2** that you might fear the LORD your God, to keep all his statutes and his commandments, which I command you, you, and your son, and your son's son, all the days of your life; and that your days may be prolonged. **Deuteronomy 6:4-7** Hear, Israel: The LORD is our God; the LORD is one: **6:5** and you shall love the LORD your God with all your heart, and with all your soul, and with all your might. **6:6** These words, which I command you this day, shall be on your heart; **6:7** and you shall teach them diligently to your children, and shall talk of them when you sit in your house, and when you walk by the way, and when you lie down, and when you rise up. **Proverbs 13:22** A good man leaves an inheritance to his children's children, but the wealth of the sinner is stored for the righteous. **Matthew 18:5-6** Whoever receives one such little child in my name receives me, **18:6** but whoever causes one of these little ones who believe in me to stumble, it would be better for him that a huge millstone should be hung around his neck, and that he should be sunk in the depths of the sea. **Ephesians 6:4** You fathers, don't provoke your children to wrath, but nurture them in the discipline and instruction of the Lord. **Colossians 3:21** Fathers, don't provoke your children, so that they won't be discouraged. **Proverbs 22:15** Folly is bound up in the heart of a child: the rod of discipline drives it far from him. **Proverbs 22:6** Train up a child in the way he should go, and when he is old he will not depart from it.

Pitfall

7

Cutting Communication Lines

Cutting communication lines is a *Pitfall* many find themselves in. You might already be in it. Not keeping communication lines open—*really open*—will *not* help you right now. When you cut the lines of communication, you are isolating yourself from real help, from real healing, from real wholeness.

There are five major communication lines you *don't* want to cut. You want these to be open—*really open*.

The FIRST line of communication is: *to yourself.*

You might be saying, *"Oh, trust me, I talk to myself all the time about this separation. I can't get it out of my head!*" Ok, we'll agree with you, but what line are you keeping open? Is it the negative, "relive the worst, be wounded by every problem" type of line? Or is it the "I'll get through this, I'll find solutions, do the best, think the best" type of line?

Self-talk is very powerful in everyday living. It seems to take on new dimensions when we find ourselves going through a major crisis. Separation is your major crisis, and it seems to be breeding more crises! There's a lot of chatter going on up there in your head, and only *you* can control what's being said.

An ancient Chinese proverb states: "*That the birds fly overhead, this you cannot stop. That they build a nest in your hair, this you can prevent.*"

There are thoughts that you seemingly can't control. They fly by, out of nowhere. But allowing them to *stay* there as you dwell on them and have emotions over them, that you *can* control. Those who have properly gone through separation have repeatedly stated that it was this controlling of their thoughts that gave them some of their greatest victories. *Not* doing so yielded a life of much greater anxiety and frustration.

> "*I remember how angry I would get while doing the laundry, the dishes, or anytime my mind was pretty much idol. I would begin thinking about what my soon-to-be ex had yelled at me, how unfair he was with his verbal attacks on me. I would see and hear it over and over in my head, like a stuck video that just kept replaying the same scenes over and over. The more I relived those thoughts, the angrier I became. Half the time I put too much detergent in the stupid wash because of it! Was I paying attention to what I*

was doing? No, I had to dwell on his words, his posturing, his anger!"

Vicky – Kansas City, MO

"The day that she told me she wanted a divorce was the day I knew it was really going to end. The last three years we were barely hanging on. The yelling, the coolness, the anger, the silence—it was all coming to a head. But then it got ugly. The lies she told to her family and friends about me sent me through the roof. How could she do that? The truth was bad enough, but to add lies to make me look worse was too much. I kept asking, Why? Why? And then I began plotting my own plan of attacks; thinking about all the ways to get back at her became my all-consuming thoughts. During work hours, on break, driving home—it was driving me crazy! My mind was non-stop on reliving how she hurt me!"

Jake – Albany, NY

It really is a choice—*your* choice. Which line of communication to yourself will you keep open? You make that choice every time a "bird of negative thought" flies by.

No one said it's easy. But after training yourself to control what you will and won't think about, it *will* become easier. God is there to help you through this process, but He gave us free will and the ability to choose. Choosing *not* to think about certain things and replacing them with thoughts that are positive, pure, and right is really what the process entails. The end results make a huge difference.

"There it was in a book I had bought years ago. I wasn't looking for it, but one day while passing by my

bookshelves in my ever-cluttered home office, there it was, and I pulled it out. It had given me a lot of confidence when I needed it years ago when I was first starting my home business. I was so unsure back then. Full of hope mixed with fear and inexperience.

"The chapter on: Thinking your way to the top, was of special interest. It was the first time I started to think about what I thought about. Back then, it made me think about success, and especially me succeeding. It made a difference. A huge difference. I had succeeded! And thinking correctly helped me get there. I smiled remembering those earlier days.

"Coming back to the soberness of my present life, I knew I had succeeded in business, but my married life had failed. The book and that chapter on 'thinking' made me think again. No, I wasn't going to succeed in this marriage, nor did either of us want to, but I was alarmed how I had let my thought life become so destructive. This separation had made me a real 'hate thinker' toward you-know-who, and I let it happen!

"I stayed right there and re-read that chapter. That was when my turning point came. When once again I chose not to dwell and live with such destructive, negative thoughts, day in and day out."

Samantha – San Diego, CA

"'It's a matter of deciding not to think about all that bad stuff,' he told me as we sat over coffee at our favorite local diner. 'It used to control my every thought, thinking what she did to me, and until I stopped allowing myself such continuous mental warfare, it just kept on going!' I sat there listening, watching his facial expressions and his body language

as he described his Divorce from Hell, which he had just gotten through only ten months earlier. He was a great friend. I had taught him how to play racquetball in college and now, sadly, he was teaching me a better way to do separation. I was not doing well, and he was showing some much better moves for me to take.

"It's a matter of deciding not to think about all that bad stuff."

Parker – Columbia, SC

Communication lines are open to yourself, yes, but *which ones*? Making a conscious effort to minimize, not dwell on or feed those thoughts that you know are not healthy will get you to a much more objective, stronger mindset that you need now more than ever!

The SECOND line of communication is: *to your spouse.*

This gets mixed reviews every time it's mentioned. Some of you are not speaking at *all* to your significant other, while others have daily phone calls and personal conversations, some even seeing each other multiple times a day. It runs the entire spectrum.

To be quite honest, for some of you *less* communication with your spouse is actually best right now. Talking gets you and the situation to the boiling point. But notice that I said *less* communication, not *none*. We know all about the pain and the flare-ups and the anger and the emotions that can come about with a simple phone call, let alone a real eye-to-eye conversation.

What we're talking about is the willingness to keep trying, to keep the lines of communication open despite the pain and the frustration. They might be shorter in length, but you still have conversations. You might do it less, but you keep the emails answered. You might not invite the other inside the house, but you'll talk to them at the front door—the *opened* front door.

> *"I remember how every time I tried calling her, all she would do is hang up once she realized it was me. That was so frustrating! And she did that until the day we got our divorce! It would have taken so little to be heard, but she wouldn't even allow me that. A two-way conversation? That would have been a miracle in itself. All I wanted was for her to hear me out. Whether it was something to do with one of our two kids or something going on with us. She totally shut me out, and nothing can convince me that helped. It came back to her one way or another, especially when the court proceedings started. I fought her even harder on stuff I could have cared less on. Still, today, two years later, I get angry just thinking about it. My advice? Don't do that to another person, let alone the one you were married to and had children with. It's so destructive. So unhealthy."*
>
> ### Kevin – Macon, GA

> *"'It's over,' he would say and just shake his head looking downward. 'Ok,' I said, 'but can't we talk about it?' 'Nothing to talk about,' he would say. 'There's a lot to talk about,' I countered. But he was shutting me out. Not even open to the possibility we could work this out. I wasn't going to give up. I had invested too much in these twenty-two years of marriage. We talked about what the kids were up to, what was next on the school schedule, who would pick up who, when. But he never wanted to talk about us. At first I showed anger at his resistance. Then I grew to be patient. It wasn't easy, but I kept talking about*

everything else but us, just to keep the doors open. I asked about his work, his car, his golf game. I knew others didn't have half of what we had in keeping the communication doors open, by just talking. It finally paid off.

"Seven months into our separation, he was beginning to open up about how he saw us, where we had gone wrong. It was amazing. I almost let on how incredibly excited I was that he was initiating some real conversation about us, our past, even our future. We're still separated, but divorce seems further from happening. I am so grateful for this chance we have together. It's slow. Painfully so. But we're talking. Talking about us."

Julie – Dayton, OH

Keeping the communication lines open to your spouse will be an ongoing challenge, and while some view it as a way to maintain the separation in a more healthy way, for others it will be the very tool leading them back to their spouse. Yes, reconciliation.

For some of you that is exactly what you are hoping for, praying for, longing for – to get back together with your spouse. But for others the thought of even the possibility of reconciling sounds scary, unsettling, or even impossible, yet getting closer to your spouse is ultimately the ideal goal God would have for you. Will that happen to *you*? Maybe not, but being open to the possibility has actually led some couples to eventually work their way back to reconciliation and togetherness. Now again, even if that's the last thing you want to happen, don't close off communication. My wife, Kathy, and I have seen *"openness to the possibility of reconciliation"* happen to couples. Not many, but enough to know that communication is the foundation. Communicating with your spouse is the "right" thing to do even if it doesn't always "feel" good. Even if they don't do it back to you.

Reconciliation is ultimately the best for you and your family, but we know it doesn't always happen. It didn't with either of us, me or Kathy. But we know being open to it while still being in the separation phase is a healthy, biblical approach to this crazy time you're experiencing. There are some great books which focus completely on this issue of reconciliation and what others have done to see it happen. We hope you seriously consider reading one and asking God to guide you as you do.

But no matter where you stand on the issue of reconciliation, *communication with your spouse* is vital for plenty of other reasons. We hope you do your part in making communication happen. You'll be glad you did.

The THIRD line of communication is: *to your family.*

This includes both the immediate and extended varieties. Don't shut out the ones who care most, be it your children, your mom and dad, or your brothers or sisters.

Keeping the lines open doesn't mean you have to take their advice, but what it does mean is that you are part of them and they you. That this is a time of crisis and you are open, available. You need them for support emotionally and possibly even materially with housing, food, transportation, or money. They want to help, whether you were to ask or not. The issue isn't so much about your material needs as it is the *open lines* so they can know how you're doing. If your needs do come up, that's another issue. The emphasis is on *open communication.*

"I was so embarrassed when I was going through my divorce. From the time my family found out about our separation, I didn't even call them. They were out of state and I hadn't seen much of my brothers or sisters through most of my married life, so I didn't feel especially close enough to contact them. But worst of all was the fact that I was the first person to be getting a divorce in our extended family.

"And I was the only Christian! It was really humbling. I had failed at marriage, and yet I had told them about God and Heaven over the years. I felt like a hypocrite. There was so much of the marriage they never knew about. Our marriage was peaceful. Simply no communication at all, practically. We loved our kids. Our marital status was a quiet, smiles-on-faces, empty-inside type of existence. We had perfected it nicely. But its outcome destroyed our marriage.

"After nearly a year of separation from my wife, one of my friends kept encouraging me to contact my extended family. She kept saying, 'Talk to your brothers and sisters, open up, they care and want to hear from you.' Her persistent, gentle approach finally saw a positive turn of events. I chose to call each of my family members all in one day. To say hi, to say I missed them. To say I just wanted to get back in touch. Their warm welcome was so wonderful. So…surprising. No harsh judgments, no deep questions about the separation. Each in their own way, gave me a reassurance of their love and that they were there if I needed to talk, visit, or anything. My friend's advice took a while to sink in but helped me deeply when I needed it most."

Sid – Gardena, CA

"At first I simply told them it would be okay, just that their father and I needed some space to work things out. Of course, it was much more serious than that. Being only five and seven, their world was much different than our adult one, so it bought me some time. But days became weeks and weeks ran into months. Daddy's less frequent visits were taking their toll. I needed to talk more openly, still at their level, but openly. At first I was going to do it myself, but in my reading I had learned the importance, for the children, to have both parents present when talking to the kids about separation. So that's what we did. It was hard. I still can see the disbelief, the tears, the slow pain of reality take hold of each of their faces. Daddy and Mommy were breaking up.

"I was committed to keep the communication open between me and the kids and not let them keep unresolved feelings deep inside. I periodically asked them leading questions. I would hold them as I answered. I re-assured them this was not their doing; that both Daddy and Mommy loved them deeply and always will. I'm not sure how much my husband talks to them, but I'm committed to doing so."

Faye – Sarasota, FL

The age of your children will also determine what works best when trying to talk to them during this separation phase. There are some excellent resources available to guide you in your approach. **Shanna** learned one technique the old-fashioned way: on her own.

"I tried asking questions, to make sure he was alright about things, but it wasn't working. He would just say 'Fine' or 'I'm OK,' never really telling me his true feelings. He missed his Dad, and Dad was rarely coming by. I soon realized through trial and error I needed to do more than just occasionally ask, 'How

*are things?' I learned I needed to just 'hang out' with
my teenage son and by doing so, not asking him
questions about his feelings, he would eventually
talk—at his pace, on his time. I remember sitting for
hours watching him work on some school project or
watching him work out with weights downstairs in the
basement. Just being there, talking about other stuff,
he would eventually begin to share and talk about the
separation. It's a secret technique this mom doesn't
keep secret!"*

Shanna – Gatlinburg, TN

The FOURTH line of communication is: *to your
friends.*

For many of us, our circle of friends for many years
has been dominated by married couples or same-sex
friends who are married, whether or not your mate
knows their mate. It's a world of "*marrieds*"! Then you
find yourself separated, and you feel like a third wheel
with other couples.

It's just not the same. They are gracious to invite
you over for a meal or to go out with you, but it's
awkward. You know it. They know it. So after a while
you start to simply pull back from those couple-type
encounters.

When you meet with same-sex friends who are
married, you find they easily share their opinion with
you, even if they can't really relate, not having been
separated or divorced, but they will jump on the
bandwagon and agree with the rightness of your hatred
or be a soft listener in your pain. But they can't really
relate. You start to withdraw.

For some it might be embarrassment. You have the stigma of a failed marriage, and you can't face them. They might look down on you, judge you, or feel pity for you, none of which you want right now. So you pull away.

Can you think of friends you've pulled away from? This is not unusual, but don't go to extremes.

*"When she wanted out of the marriage after only being together for fourteen months, I was in shock. I had waited later than most of my friends to get married, because I had seen so many end in divorce. When it came my turn to choose a marriage partner, I was going to be sure I was getting the right one! So when we did get married, after I let all those years go by, I didn't want to wait to have kids. She got pregnant that first month. Now they both were out of my life, and I was stunned with the reality that the very thing I had planned **not** to happen had happened! It sent me into isolation. It was my way of dealing with the pain.*

"Every night for over a year I would come straight home after work, come in, close the curtains, and begin my ritual of going on the computer or watch TV, all that time thinking she would come to her senses and walk through that door with our daughter. I shut everyone out waiting for that to happen.

"Slowly, I mean slowly, I started to come out of my shell, my cave, my protective surroundings. Where had the time gone? How could I have cut everyone off like I had? Yes, they had tried, many repeatedly, to reach me, but I kept distant. After a while everyone gave up on me. Just what I had wanted. Or so I thought. But I thought wrong, and now, as I work myself back into relationships with past friends, I can

*only warn others not to be so inward with your pain.
Friends can really help, if only to hear you out."*
Josh – Santa Monica, CA

"*Hearing you out*" is one great gift a friend can give you during this phase of marital separation, but for many of your friends, it's just too much. They can't relate or they begin to avoid you knowing the only thing you will talk about is your pain and the details of your battle. Some, like **Fran**, do find those special friends to share with—but she knows not all of her friends will react the same, so she opens up *selectively* with certain ones. With the others, she simply has other friendly conversations, avoiding the deeper issues of her separation. Those thoughts and emotions she saves for only a few.

"We were the best of friends. We went to college together—as roommates. Did the student government activities together. Double dated. It was a great time. After college we both took jobs in the same city, and we took on the town living a single's life! Boy, did we learn a lot! She got married first, but I got pregnant first! We still had breakfast together at least once a week, like we had when we were both single. Those were important times of sharing, laughing, crying. Those times together bonded us in our ever-changing lives.

"When my husband left me for other 'pursuits' on his climb to the top in his corporation, the whole conversation focused on me and him. Her listening ear was so needed then. I would just pour out my heart to her. My disillusionments, my fears, my uncertainties. She was incredible. She was there to listen, not so much to agree with me. She was amazing. I never felt judged by her, and she always asked me such probing

questions to help me understand myself better. After eight months of my separation being on and off again, my husband and I finally found some real help in counseling. He and I still go there every Thursday night. It's been worth the cost.

"He's back home. Things are looking better. My friend and I still meet for breakfast!"

Fran – Eugene, OR

The FIFTH line of communication is: *to your God.*

Have you cut the communication line to God? Be honest with yourself. It's one thing to know He's there and occasionally thank Him over a meal. But are you communicating with Him? Are you open to Him communicating His thoughts to you?

We learn His thoughts through His Word, the Scriptures, and by the indwelling Holy Spirit He gives to each believer. We can choose to know or not know His Word. We can choose to yield to the Holy Spirit or quench His leading. The choice of being open to God is daily—moment to moment. He should be the one we *especially* seek out.

For when all is said and done, no one can fully relate, divorced or not, to your situation like God can. He sees all, knows all. That includes you. He is fully acquainted with all your ways, your thoughts, your desires, your fears, your joys, your pain, your hopes. He's God. Only God can be *fully* aware of those things in your life.

When you sleep, when you awaken, when you eat breakfast, when you're driving, when you are in meetings, running errands, picking kids up, putting kids to bed—He is there. 24/7 and 365 days a year, plus one for leap years—He's always there. Caring, concerned, forgiving, strengthening, directing, approving, correcting, loving, providing—He's there.

He's God.

He's not cutting the line of communication with you. He's always present with a listening ear. It's about you with Him, not Him with you. Will you come back if you've wandered off and stay back every day with Him? He'll help you to do that. Simply talk to Him about it. Simply keep the line of communication open. You know you'll be glad you did!

"It was the worst time of my married life, of my life, period. After eight years of marriage, his lifestyle and mine were at direct odds. With children in the picture, I especially wanted some spiritual values for them, something my husband and I never much thought of when it was just us. But now the kids were old enough to understand right and wrong. I wanted God to be there early on for them. My husband thought I was pushing religion down their throats. 'Going to Sunday school once a week is hardly pushing,' I said.

"His lack of interest and my growing interest in God only added to our drifting apart. But in the end, it was my renewed walk with God, learning His ways, that helped me through our marriage problems, and we did find real help in the years that followed. Though still not a Christian, my husband is attending church with me and the kids. It's slow, but I'm encouraged to see God working!"

Courtney – Brooklyn, NY

"I knew I needed God's help. A friend of mine invited me to church, but it was more than just church that I needed. I wanted a real, everyday relationship with God that was meaningful and growing deeper! Going to church was the start of it. It was there I learned how to really know God personally. The difference is so real. My friends still can't believe how much stronger I am. My problems didn't go away, but my ability to work through them did change—thanks to God."

Bennett – Montgomery, AL

This can be a long journey on this road of separation. Having someone like God walking with you through it, can only be best for you and for all that surround you. Others who have gone on before you have found the wisdom in doing just that. It's our prayer that you, too, will embrace a daily walk with the One who knows and cares for you like no other.

Cutting communication lines to yourself, your spouse, your family, your friends, and your God is *not* a *Pitfall* you want to experience. What choices do you need to make today to once again open these lines of communication? You *can* do this! We ourselves eventually did. Now it's your turn. We pray you do.

Scriptural Insights: Ch.7
Cutting Communication Lines

Psalm 15:2 He who walks blamelessly does what is right, and speaks truth in his heart **Philippians 4:8** Finally, brothers, whatever things are true, whatever things are honorable, whatever things are just, whatever things are pure, whatever things are lovely, whatever things are of good report; if there is any virtue, and if there is any praise, think about these things. **Zechariah 8:16** These are the things that you shall do: speak every man the truth with his neighbor. Execute the judgment of truth and peace in your gates **Colossians 1:9** For this cause, we also, since the day we heard this, don't cease praying and making requests for you, that you may be filled with the knowledge of his will in all spiritual wisdom and understanding **James 1:5** But if any of you lacks wisdom, let him ask of God, who gives to all liberally and without reproach; and it will be given to him. **Psalm 52:3** You love evil more than good, lying rather than speaking the truth. **Ephesians 4:15** but speaking truth in love, we may grow up in all things into him, who is the head **Ephesians 4:25** Therefore, putting away falsehood, speak truth each one with his neighbor. For we are members of one another. **1 Corinthians 13:4-5** Love is patient and is kind; love doesn't envy. Love doesn't brag, is not proud, **13:5** doesn't behave itself inappropriately, doesn't seek its own way, is not provoked, takes no account of evil **Matthew 7:11** If you then, being evil, know how to give good gifts to your children, how much more will your Father who is in heaven give good things to those who ask him! **John 3:11a** Most certainly I tell you, we speak that which we know, and testify of that which we have seen **Psalm 40:17** But I am poor and needy. May the Lord think about me. You are my help and my deliverer. Don't delay, my God. **Psalm 34:12-13** Who is someone who desires life, and loves many days, that he may see good? **34:13** Keep your tongue from evil, and your lips from speaking lies. **Psalm 141:3** Set a watch, LORD, before my mouth. Keep the door of my lips. **Proverbs 4:24** Put away from yourself a perverse mouth. Put corrupt lips far from you. **Proverbs 15:2** The tongue of the wise commends knowledge, but the mouth of fools gush out folly. **Proverbs 15:7** The lips of the wise spread knowledge; not so with the heart of fools. **Proverbs 15:23** Joy comes to a man with the reply of his mouth. How good is a word at the right time! **Proverbs 15:28** The heart of the righteous weighs answers, but the mouth of the wicked gushes out evil. **Proverbs 16:27** A worthless man devises mischief. His speech is like a scorching fire. **Proverbs 18:7** A fool's mouth is his destruction, and his lips are a snare to his soul. **Ephesians 4:29** Let no corrupt speech proceed out of your mouth, but such as is good for building up as the need may be, that it may give grace to those who hear. **James 1:19** So, then, my beloved brothers, let every man be swift to hear, slow to speak, and slow to anger; **James 3:8-10** But nobody can tame the tongue. It is a restless evil, full of deadly poison. **3:9** With it we bless our God and Father, and with it we curse men, who are made in the image of God. **3:10** Out of the same mouth comes forth blessing and cursing. My brothers, these things ought not to be so. **Jeremiah 29:11** For I know the thoughts that I think toward you, says the LORD, thoughts of peace, and not of evil, to give you hope and a future.

SocietyD.com
When You
Separate or Divorce

Conclusion

You did it! You successfully read about the *7 Painful Pitfalls to Avoid* while *Separated But Not Divorced.* You have just completed something Kathy and I never had the chance to read. It would have saved us from so much pain and so many bad decisions. We hope you will refer to these in the near future, and we ask you to review, one more time, each *Pitfall* before you leave us.

Pitfall #1 – A Support Group? Not Now, Maybe Later

Pitfall #2 – Opposite Sex Relationships—Yes, If They Help You!

Pitfall #3 – Making Major Decisions *Before* Gaining Objectivity

Pitfall #4 – Separation Symptoms? I'm Not Aware of Any!

Pitfall #5 – Not Deepening your Spiritual Roots

Pitfall #6 – My Kids Are Fine—Kids Bounce Back!

Pitfall #7 – Cutting Communication Lines

Now, for a final exercise, may we suggest you glance over this list and prioritize them according to what you need to begin working on most? Just grab a pen, or do this in your mind, and next to each *Pitfall* begin with what could be the #1 area to really give priority, and then mark the rest 2-7 in order of importance. Yes, they could all be #1 or #2, but this will give you a general sense of the *Pitfalls* you are most concerned with, right now, in your life of separation. Just stop and do this, then come back.

Welcome back! Ranking that list can really help. In whatever order you prioritized the *Pitfalls*, it's all about choices. Being *aware*, and then taking *action*. You're now aware, so really it's a matter of action, *you* taking action.

We hope the best for you along the way, for the road of separation *is* full of *Pitfalls*. We've mentioned some key ones. Knowing about them is vitally important. They can make a difference; we hope they have, we hope they will.

Our prayers go with you as you continue this journey. We'd love to hear about your progress. Email us any time! Simply visit **www.FallonBooks.com** and go to the *"Contact Us"* icon. Be sure to come by our website: **www.SocietyD.com** . . . It's worth visiting!

- Sincerely—Gary & Kathy and everyone whose life contributed to this book.

P.S. Do you know someone who could use this book? We've made an easy way for you to share it with them! (*Please see last page*)

Notes

Introduction

1.Pitfall. (n.d.). *The American Heritage® Dictionary of the English Language, Fourth Edition.* Retrieved August 30, 2006, from Dictionary.com website:
http://dictionary.reference.com/search?q=pitfall

2.Pitfall. (n.d.). *WordNet® 2.0.* Retrieved August 30, 2006, from Dictionary.com website:
http://dictionary.reference.com/search?q=pitfall

Pitfall # 1

1.Steve Grissom, *DivorceCare Workbook*, (Wake Forest, NC: The Church Initiative, Inc, 2004) p. v.

2. Support group. (n.d.). *The American Heritage® Dictionary of the English Language, Fourth Edition.* Retrieved August 30, 2006, from Dictionary.com website:
http://dictionary.reference.com/search?q=support group&x=30&y=13

3.Support group. (n.d.). *Merriam-Webster's Medical Dictionary.* Retrieved August 30, 2006, from Dictionary.com website:
http://dictionary.reference.com/search?q=support group&x=30&y=13

4.Divorce Recovery Workshop benefits (www.drw.org.uk, 6/26/04).

Pitfall # 2

1.Steve Grissom, *DivorceCare Video*, (Wake Forest, NC: The Church Initiative, Inc, 2004) Session 7. Dr. Jim Talley is an international author who heads Relationship Resources, a counseling ministry based in Oklahoma City. His interview quotes are seen on many of the DivorceCare Videos.

2.Ibid.

3.Tigerx.com/trivia/stress.htm

Pitfall # 4

1.Michael S. Gottlieb, *AIDS at 25: I knew Patient Zero* The doctor's report of June 5, 1981, would mark the official onset of the epidemic. Michael S. Gottlieb teaches at UCLA's medical school where he is affiliated with the AIDS Institute. He is a trustee of the Global AIDS Interfaith Alliance (www.thegaia.org). June 5, 2006.
www.latimes.com/news/printedition/opinion/la-oe-gottlieb5jun05,1,7446223.story

Malcom Gladwell, *The Tipping Point: How Little Things Can Make a Big Difference*, Back Bay Books Reprint Edition (January 7, 2002) p. 21.

2.Tigerx.com/trivia/stress.htm

Pitfall # 6

1.Judith S. Wallerstein, Julia M. Lewis, Sandra Blakeslee, *The Unexpected Legacy of Divorce: A 25-Year Landmark Study,* Hyperion (September 6, 2000)

Judith S. Wallerstein, Sandra Blakeslee, *What About the Kids?*, Hyperion; 1st Edition (March 12, 2003)

Elizabeth Marquardt, *Between Two Worlds*,
Random House Inc (2005)

2.Tigerx.com/trivia/stress.htm

3.Steve Grissom, *DivorceCare Video*, (Wake Forest, NC: The Church Initiative, Inc, 2004) p. 74.

Unless otherwise indicated, all Scripture quotations are taken from the World English Bible which is a Modern English update of American Standard Version of 1901. This translation is in the Public Domain.

References and quotes from DivorceCare materials are used by permission.

A Special Thanks...

To some very special friends Kathy and I have met along the way of our ongoing journey in this ministry of separation and divorce recovery. Some worked with us side by side in ministering to those who went through separation or divorce. Some gave us counsel, insight, prayer and friendship along our way. This book is a big part of their doing and words can never express our gratitude of how our Lord used them in our life and continues to do so. Keep praying for us. We have a lot more to do to help those who are where we once were.

Our love and thanks goes out to:

Steve Grissom, Pastor John Chinelly, Pastor Bob Coy, Ken and Peggy Banks, Alan Metzger, Diana Hines, Lelah Lynch, Stephanie Fey, Michael Keenan, David Moss, David Utley, Carol Whiteman, Tom Miner, Gary Becherer, Joe Garcia, Gayle Pritchard, Laurie Engelhardt, John Dillavou, Penny Pearlman, Cary Hollingsworth, Linda Lubinsky, Lorna Spence, Marie Miranda, Helena Benitez, Kay Harker, Don and Carol Miller, Ron Johnson, Ernie Martin, Ray and Haydee Traver, Bonnie Mathias, John and Kathy Weber, Bob Discipio, Cheryl Sauvage, Naomi Ford, Joseph Northcut, Pastor Chet Lowe, Pastor Bernard King, Pastor Greg Howard, Pat Baird, Warren and Cheryl Kniskern and the many facilitators and attendees during the years of ministry Kathy and I have had the honor to be with. To our extended and immediate families and especially our 5 great children, Carrie, Jeremy, Candace, Nialls and Cory, who went through our journeys of Separation and Divorce, we give our love. Our *greatest gratitude* is to God. He is the great Healer, Redeemer, Almighty, and truly caring, forgiving Lord.

SocietyD.com

When You
Separate or Divorce

It's worth visiting . . .

Gary and Kathy Fallon
Founders

Author's Note

Do you know someone who could use this book?

We've created a customized email that you can use which quickly informs others about this book!

A simple email with details about our book, *Separated but Not Divorced,* is a few key strokes away!

It's fast and easy. Simply go to our website:

www.FallonBooks.com

- This is a great way to pass this book along to a friend in a convenient, informative manner.
- They will see the Book cover with links on learning more about the contents.
- You can write your personal message with the email so they know it's from you to them.
- It's a customized book recommendation email – It looks great!
- It really is fast and easy!

We hope you decide to do this for your friends.
They will go at their pace to decide what to do next,
but at least they now know where to find answers.
Thanks for sharing this book with others!

CONTACTING THE AUTHORS

To contact us, simply visit our website:
www.FallonBooks.com and press the "*Contact Us*" icon.

Be sure to visit our website: **www.SocietyD.com**
It's worth visiting!

9 781595 264404